Rosa, a Survivor

A VICTIM OF TERRORISM
SHE FINDS PURPOSE OF LIFE
AND LOVE IN A NEW WORLD

"What a lovely place. What a lovely face"
'Hotel California' - by the Rock Eagles group

Daniel J. Verin

ISBN 979-8-218-08118-8

'Rosa, a survivor' is a work of fiction.

All incidents and dialogues, and all characters are products of the author's imagination and are not to be construed as real.

Any resemblance to actual persons, living or dead, is entirely coincidental.

In the Sahara Desert she suffered the horrors of terrorism.

Escaping to the end of the world,

in Baja California, she frees herself from her PTSD nightmares,

finds love and new purposes to her life.

Introduction

Dear readers,

Dedicated to all victims of all armed conflicts, this book, the second of the Henry Towers series, was written to raise you awareness about the traumatic effects of terrorism, while telling you a story with a happy ending.

The novel is about an episode in the life of Rosa Vasquez, an archaeologist defender of indigenous women, as she was running away from the PTSD pains that she, alone, knew.

Let me share with you how I happened to meet Rosa and how I ended up writing this book. It covers the first two years she spent in Baja California, from 2013 to 2015, while she searched and found peace, after a life of traumas on three continents.

Two years ago, in March 2018, I received a call from Bob Harding, a friend of mine who is Chair at the San Diego University Department of History.

"Hey, Henry, would you like to contribute to our summer lecture series on 'Colonialism and Anti-Colonialism'? You sure know a lot about Algeria, before and after its independence from France. You spent so much time there. And you have so many contacts and friends on both sides of the rift that developed there, since the disastrous colonial adventure of the nineteenth century. Please accept our invitation. I'd very much like to see you again. So, do you agree?"

Needless to say, I was more than happy to leave my Washington D.C. apartment, during the usual hot-and-humid summer. Delightful San Diego sounded like heaven-on-earth.

At the end of the last session, a researcher came to see me back-stage. She looked quite sharp. Bright eyed and passionate. But not your usual twenty-some, anymore. Was she hiding some trauma?

"My name is Rosa. Rosa Vasquez. I live in Baja but I am working on a research project in the Anthropology Department, under Professor Conway. When I was at the Sorbonne, a long time ago, working on my PhD thesis, I had the pleasure to read your book 'the Torch' about the World War 2 American landing in North Africa."

She spoke English quite fluently but with an unusual accent that was not fully French, yet close to it.

"I was then in Algeria where I was documenting my first book, based on my doctoral thesis 'Berber Women of Algeria'. She continued with anxiety "I know a lot about that country ..."

As she was saying those few words, I was surprised to hear her voice turn into a mumbled whisper mixed with a weird stammer.

For a moment, I felt awkward, sensing in her something deeper than plain shyness. Was she trying to hide something? I wanted to give her a chance to go on with her introduction. "Yes?" said I.

That was enough for her to overcome her brief hesitation. "I am Algerian, you see. Specializing in prehistoric cave paintings ... In North Africa. And now in the Americas ..."

After a short pause, she continued "... I want to identify links between the social life and psychology of primitive humans and modern indigenous people. I believe that indigenous women, especially in Baja California, still possess hidden human qualities that the rest of the world has forgotten or lost ... and should now recover or relearn, before it's too late."

Her enthusiasm and clarity of mind were remarkable. Yet, her voice was burdened with what seemed to be an overwhelming anxiety.

You can understand my surprise when she suddenly asked me to write a book about her own life experiences. "I want to let the world know about my story ... I cannot possibly do it myself ... I love your direct style ... You would be perfect ... Please?"

Stunned by her abrupt request and her insistence, I agreed to be her ghost-writer. First, out of sheer curiosity. Then, as time went by, I became fascinated by her personality and the richness of her unique life. Rosa wanted to focus only on the 2013 to 2015 period, when a major event happened, after she moved to and settled in Baha.

It is only later that I realized that Rosa is an exemplary survivor in a world tormented by tensions that demented groups decided to resolve by exacting terrorist acts on innocent people.

To work on that unexpected project, I decided to stay two more weeks at the San Diego Fairmont Grand Del Mar hotel overlooking the Pacific Ocean.

During the last week of July 2018, Rosa came from her Piedra del Sol university residence, to visit me daily for long and intense work sessions.

Using her fancy-dancy IPAD to record our conversations and my well-tested old-fashioned paper and pencil technology, we went through the project's first phase: listening to Rosa's recollections and taking notes about her fascinating life.

At the end of this preliminary work, Rosa insisted that we pay a visit to Doctor Claire Caldwell, the Navy Medical Centre psychiatrist specialized in Posttraumatic Stress Disorder (PTSD), who had treated her for three months in the spring of 2013 – without any positive result. "A difficult case," she confided.

Doctor Caldwell's hesitating comment helped me understand both the seriousness of Rosa's condition and the reason why she had stopped her therapy to get a research job at the University.

Each time I tried to invite Rosa to share the cause of her psychological pains, she would bristle and categorically refuse to talk. I was puzzled, though. To please me, she would sometimes mention the Eagles Rock Group's musically genial song 'Hotel California.' As if under the spell, her tensions gone, she sounded mesmerized while humming the beautiful tune or going over its lyrics.

Before we left San Diego, a communications student helped Rosa buy professional cameras for her Baja-California rock paintings research project that she was organizing for a group of young Cochimi Amerindians in search of their ancestors' artworks.

Once finished with our preparations, on a bright morning already too hot to my taste, here we were driving south towards the nearby border with Mexico. After two days of driving 1000 miles along the increasingly deserted Baja-California peninsula, we arrived in Todos Santos. Rosa was ecstatic to be back with her family, her husband, and her twin boys.

I spent a whole month working in Todos Santos. While absorbing the beauty of that fascinating land and the human qualities of its people, I tried to figure out how a university professor like Rosa could have chosen such a small tropical town, delightful yet so isolated.

As a self-respecting American tourist, I let Carlos, Rosa's husband, convince me to have a drink or two at the Hotel California. You may know that this is the local hotel that became famous for its legal problems with the rock band "The Eagles" around their famous title of the same name. I had a lot of fun chatting with Carlos. The little Spanish I knew, and his bits of English allowed us to work and have a good time. A Native American, friendly, and talkative, he wanted to make sure that I had an intimate knowledge of the precious details of Rosa's extraordinary life in Todos Santos, the reactions of the residents to her arrival and her contributions to the city's life.

After several days of informal conversations, Carlos gave me a copy of the voluminous notes he had taken during the shamanic hypnosis sessions for Rosa's healing. It is then that I began to understand her secret.

After the work with Carlos was done, Rosa asked me to put a funny spin on the description of her four nights of hypnosis. Imagining herself as a new Shahrazad, she wanted me to follow the style of the 'Arabian Nights' a bit.

Big order!

"Let me tell you, Henry. You'll understand, I'm sure," she explained. "For my seventh birthday, my mother gave me an illustrated version of the so-called 'Arabian Tales' which, in fact, are not Arabian but Persian. For reasons you will understand later, the theme of the 'Arabian Nights' fits my story a little. You will see. The tales have complex turns. There are tales inside other tales. You will tell me that I only had four nights, but there are some parallels with the many more nights of Shahrazad. The premise is that Shahrazad the courtesan, survives only thanks to the continuity of her tales that she extends night after night to entertain a lecherous and criminal old sultan. A little crazy you say? No doubt. Crazy, but fitting."

After my return to Washington, using Zoom – then in its infancy - Rosa and I did manage to craft the book you are going to read. However, she decided to never read Chapter 2 derived from Carlos's notes.

As you follow her adventures, you might catch shocking glimpses of recent international historical events.

And perhaps, driven in the ripping currents of a world in constant change, you might re-learn some age-old lessons about what it means to be human.

Henry Towers, May 30, 2020

Table of Contents

CHAPTER 1

Life in dreamland.

LANDING AT LOS CABOS – Nov 15, 2013

"OK, lady, up we go!"

The single-engine Cessna pilot obviously cultivates his just-past-sixty macho image. Worn out captain cap tipped sideways, gold-framed airman sunglasses, garish Hawaiian shirt. The works.

According to his well-honed routine, as soon as his 'bird' is off the airstrip, he launches his monologue, hoping to get some feedback from his captive audience. On this flight, though, he is pissed. The only passenger, on the second row, is that unassuming, smart-looking middle-aged gal. He gawks at her thru the rear-view mirror. *"Go on, man! Most of the time, shy ones like this one are the easiest to take to bed. Try! Nothing to lose ..."*

Having sized up today's situation, out of the clear blue, he starts his well-honed gig with a crack that he only considers to be funny "You know what? I cannot remember how many years I have been flying this damn San Diego to Los Cabos line. Too many weed joints packed with other yummy stuff, I guess ... you know what I mean ... Hahaha!" says he.

Then come endless monologues about his four tours of duty as a chopper pilot in Vietnam. In a glorious conclusion, he expands in gory details on his Viet Cong kill record, peppered with crass, out of context sexy jokes. At each step, while mentally preparing his saga's next snippet, he expects loud laughter and patriotic compliments.

Neatly tucked in the cabin's second row, Rosa keeps silent. Her English is too limited to even understand most of the goofy pilot's military jargon and gross flirting comments. She could not care less, anyway. Numbed by the engines' droning noise, she is overtaken by the flight's monotony. Soon, her mind starts wandering aimlessly. She would like to take charge of her thoughts. Instead, a mumble-jumble of irrational hopes and scary obsessions invade her.

The Los Cabos airport control tower gargles in the cockpit "Flight 807. You're clear for landing. Runway Two." The pilot vengefully gives the yoke a sudden jerk. Just to scare today's lone passenger out of her obnoxious silence.

—————◦/◦/◦———

Jolted upwards, Rosa mutes an instinctive gasp. Thrust against her seat belt, she manages to keep her calm.

Each time the engine speed changes for landing manoeuvres, her hypersensitivity to noise shakes her. Like a punch to the solar plexus.

—————◦/◦/◦———

She stoically follows the strict instructions she has given herself for this kind-of crazy trip: to remain incognito at all costs.

"A little bump? Who cares? Don't say a word, Rosa dear. Relax. In a minute or two you will be there. In Baja California. At the end of the earth. Away from your nightmares and your pains. Your fears will vanish. Left behind. Forever. I know. I know. Now in your fifties, you still behave like a teen-age runaway kid ... That's OK ... You had to leave."

The breath-taking bay of Los Cabos pulls her out of her foggy thoughts before the plane sharply dives towards the airport's short landing strip.

She is appalled to hear herself groan, like a cornered animal "At last. Baja," while the soothing 'Hotel California' refrain once again invades her whole being.

—————◦/◦/◦———

'What a lovely place ... What a lovely face.'

—————◦/◦/◦———

After a bouncy landing bump, the Cessna taxies on the tarmac to Terminal 2.

"Thank you, sir."

"Hey, what? You can talk? Thought you were mute or something ... Hahaha! Or maybe the little lady was too scared, up there?"

"No, not scared. Just enjoying the ride, sir."

Rosa's tone is curt and defensive. To put a quick end to any idle flirting conversation.

Unfazed, her one-time suitor goes on "All right, all right. Take it easy, sweetie. I did not mean anything wrong. There is a nice bar inside. Would you accept a drink? ... Hey, could you give a good pilot a chance to apologize?"

No doubt. The guy is an old hand at this kind of games.

"No, thank you, sir."

Rosa knows exactly what to do, as planned. *"OK, Rosa dear. Step out of the plane. Roll your two caddies. The books. The cameras. Walk as fast as you can. Casually. Straight to the Customs' window."*

———◦/◦/◦———

As she dashes to the taxi line, construction workers whistle

" Que linda! Hola, morena a donde vas tan rapido?"

[What a cutie! Hey brunette, where are you heading so fast?].

She is secretly tickled by the workers' compliment about her olive skin and long black hair. *"Well, Rosa dear. You are no Mexican. But since they call you 'morena', at least you are dark enough to blend with the locals!"*

At nine, in the mid November morning, the temp is higher than in San Diego. However, cool misty puffs of air still float inside the already oppressive heat. She arrives at the taxi line.

'Por favor, Quiero ir a Todos Santos.'

Right away the cabbie figures that she is not a local.

"Fifty bucks. One hour," he answers in English, eager to show his international savvy. Hoping for an extra tip, *Tal Vez* [maybe].

"*Gosh, no way to hide my accent!*" Rosa's amused mental self-evaluation is wrapped in a tinge of disappointment.

She keeps silent during the whole zigzagging taxi ride to Todos Santos. Flowing widely through the open window, the dry hot air hits her face in thousands of friendly smacks. The Baja wilderness. Just like what she had dreamed about at the San Diego University Library. "*Now it is the real thing. Feel Baja, dear Rosa. Become part of it – the desert, the ocean, the cacti, the sand, the rocks, the vultures … Forget about the other deserts you crossed, Rosa … Loaded with life, Baja's desert is different from what you ever imagined. This is a totally new world!*"

REAL-ESTATE DEAL IN TODOS SANTOS – Nov 15, 2013

"En esquina de la calle Cuahtemoc y la calle Zaragoza"

[To the corner of Cuahtemoc and Zaragoza streets.]

As planned, Rosa does not want the cabbie to know that she has an appointment at a real-estate agency. She gets off to roll her suitcases, waiting for the cab to be gone. Two blocks away, across from Los Pinos Park, a wooden sign proudly stands on the sidewalk

'Inmobiliaria Jiménez la mejor de Todos Santos'

Incredible as it may seem, that is where she is going to sign the deed for a beach-front hotel.

In San Diego, she had impulsively picked the ad off the real-estate Facebook page of Todos Santos' City Hall. Yes, the international EFT down-payment she made in San Diego, was way too high. Who cares? Mesmerized, she had made her decision. *"Todos Santos. A dream hotel on the beach. This will be my new place. My new life. Peaceful. Forever. Away from it all. Money is no object."*

She enters the dark real-estate office.

Shutters are closed to keep the heat from coming in and invite the flies to sneak out. Her eyes take a while to adapt to the room's darkness. The agent and a non-descript associate are having their mid-morning beer. Seated at a small folding table, they straighten themselves up to look imposing in their white suits.

'Señor Jiménez vengo por el hotel.'

[Señor Gimenez,I come for the hotel]

'Bienvenida a Todos Santos, Señora.'

The agent is pleasantly surprised to hear a foreign lady speak with such a delightful Castilian Spanish accent. To sound important, he clears his throat before going through elaborate explanations "Señor Rolando Perez is the notary public. He was assigned by the mayor's office. You see, Señora Vasquez, the property's previous owners, may God bless their souls, died without any descendants or relatives. And there has been no buyers from the locals for one year now. You know, that's because the way the owners died. That's why, Señora Vasquez, the sale is under the city's jurisdiction. And at a good price, I assure you. A beautiful beachfront property. In the very nice La Poza neighborhood. With access from Carretera Federal 19 [Highway 19]. With view to the beautiful beach and to the famous Punta Lobos. I tell you. The best of the best."

Rosa ignores some of the difficulties she has to follow the agent's rapid Mexican accent. Elated by the idea of being the owner of a beachfront Baja hotel, she does not dare pose any question about the mystery that surround the previous owners' demise. *"No use figuring details now, Rosa dear. Everything will be fine."*

Page after page, the signing formalities go without a hitch. Rosa feels good about her command of Spanish *"Well done, Rosa dear. You even understood the business terms without any difficulty! Do not worry. Your out-of-place accent will always be nothing more than a minor handicap."*

The language barrier has been easily overcome. Next on the to-do list is to create a new identity. *"That will come in time, Rosa dear. Slowly. Do not panic. Accept your limitations. No problem. Town people and future customers will soon accept you."*

What a shock, though! She silently goes over the math. *"What? 4.8 million pesos or $200,000? A 50K down payment at the San Diego Citibank office and now 150K on top of it? That's way too much! … No option, Rosa dear. Money is no object, 'member? Hide your surprise. Quell your useless anger. If there is anything wrong, it will be your fault, anyway. Agree and sign the teller's check. OK, now. Give a good impression. Paint a smile on your stupid blank face!"*

The notary public stamps and countersigns the check with all the bureaucratic decorum he can muster.

NEVER HEARD OF THAT CONSUELO! – Nov 15, 2013

With the signing formalities done, the agent ostentatiously passes a few pesos to the notary public, before telling Rosa "Here are your hotel's keys, Señora Vasquez. Now is time for me to tell you something else, Señora Vasquez: the real key to your success at the hotel will be Doña Consuelo. She will be the hotel manager, for ever. You cannot fire her."

In an instant, a painful flash of rabid anger invades Rosa's whole being. Unable to control her sudden rage, she stands up from her chair and goes into a fit, shouting "Consuelo? The hotel I am buying already has a manager? Who is that Consuelo, anyway? Nobody told me about any Consuelo!"

She is appalled to hear her own wild screeching. She is almost ready to pounce on the dumfounded agent who freezes in a pantomime posture. First agitated beyond control, she then flips into a bout of paranoia. She is certain that she is the victim of some underhanded international plot.

In a desperate effort of self-control, she decides to quell her psychotic fit. A dose of self-talk will help. She sits down, her hands folded on the table's edge. *"Remember Doctor Caldwell's advice, Rosa dear. This situation might or might not be right. But it's not worth going bonkers over it. True. I should have been told about that Consuelo before signing the papers … That's OK … Take it easy. Avoid useless theatrics. It's OK to be pissed. But no wild aggressivity, remember? No use to morph yourself into a rabid stray cat for the slightest problem, OK?"*

While Rosa relaxes in her meditative state, the shaken agent launches a syrupy theatrical explanation. "I am sorry Señora Vasquez. You have signed. You cannot change anything now. Isn't that so, Señor Perez?"

"Señor Perez!"

Awaken from his alcoholic half-sleep, the notary mumbles

"¿Qué? ¿Qué? Si, si, es verdad, legalmente".

"It's in the contract, Señora. Right there, you see Señora, in the addendum, with your signature under it. It says that you agree to keep Doña Consuelo as the La Linda manager. For ever. Oh, but do not ever worry, Señora Vasquez. I do not blame you for being upset. But in the end, you will appreciate Doña Consuelo. Everybody loves Doña Consuelo in Todos Santos. You will love her, too. She is the best hotel manager in town. She is so good that she is Don Pedro's helper. Believe you me. You are very lucky to have Doña Consuelo. I will tell you a secret: she told me that I should sell it to you and not to anyone else. Because of your name, you know. The best part of it is that, with her in charge of everything, you can be sure that no bad spirits will ever show up at Hotel La Linda!"

Apparently trying to ward off some mysterious curse, the agent furtively signs himself while mumbling "*Jesús, protégenos a todos*" [Jesus, protect us all!]. The notary public follows suit.

Rosa hesitates before answering the weird tirade. She'd like to say "*Spirits? What do you mean by spirits?*" She'd like to have the guts to calmly ask who that Don Pedro is. At a loss for words, her speech blocked by residues of anger, she stammers a platitude like "In that case, I feel much better. Anyway, I'd like to ask something else …"

The agent does not give her the chance to pose her question; and goes on with his own obfuscating theatrics "Señora Vasquez, that's perfect. I am glad you agree about Doña Consuelo. I knew that you would agree.

"Let me take care of your luggage if I may. I'll drive you to your new hotel. Straight from Carretera 19 down Calle Guaycura and from there straight to the beach. Easy, no? You are a very intelligent lady! You are from Spain, no?"

9

FIB NUMBER ONE – Nov 15, 2013

"Si. Soy realmente Española" **[Yes, I certainly am a Spaniard], answers Rosa. Her spur-of-the-moment goal is to take advantage of her first chance to hide her identity. She figures that the real-estate agent is as good a test subject as any. *"Good move, Rosa dear. This guy must be fairly prominent among the Todos Santos locals. And real-estate agents are known for launching gossiping campaigns. It's part of their marketing strategies."***

Satisfied, she gives herself a virtual pat in the back *"In no time, Rosa dear, everybody in Todos Santos will know you as 'La Española.' Not bad for a start! A little fib here. A little fib there. And nobody will know where you came from. Nor will they figure out why you came here."*

As Rosa mulls over her success, the agent comes back to the attack "Ah, I totally forgot, Señora."

"You forgot what?" Rosa is on the defensive.

"I forgot to tell you about the Fideicomiso**."**

"About the what?"

"Don't worry about it. The Fideicomiso **is a government formality. For foreigners who buy real estate in Mexico. According to your statement, please show me your Spanish passport."**

***"Dear Rosa, here you are, already tangled up,"* Rosa thinks before answering the agent, "Here is my American passport. I have a dual nationality."**

"Ah, yes? Very interesting," chuckles the agent, obviously unconvinced.

He goes to a desk to rummage in a drawer and returns with a bunch of new forms for Rosa to sign and countersign. He hesitates for a moment, before muttering " Aïe Aïe Aïe**! Consuelo will yell at me. I didn't know nothing about this dual nationality thing..."**

"Here's your passport, Senora. American, but not Gringa, right? Muy bien**. Let's go visit your wonderful property. We'll be there in a minute."**

RAMSHACKLE RUINS – Nov 15, 2013

After a short downhill ride, they arrive in front of 'the' hotel.

Second shock of the day for Rosa.

Indeed, as detailed in the ad, seen from the street, there is a gorgeous white beach in the background.

But the ramshackle structure is oddly isolated in the middle of a field of jalapeños. It is the pitiful remnant of what might have been, but certainly is not a 'dream place' as advertised nor "the best of the best" as claimed by Señor Gimenez. There is absolutely no resemblance to the jimmied Facebook picture she was flipping through her cell phone in San Diego.

A last-minute coat of army-green fresh paint still dribbles from the eaves. Windows are grossly boarded. While the real estate agent extolls the beauty of the surroundings, Rosa silently laments *"You have been fooled, Rosa dear! Two hundred thousand dollars! For a ramshackle ruin. That is absolutely not what you saw on Facebook! No problem. You will raze this mess down. In its place will soon stand the new Hotel La Linda, Baja's hidden pearl! Money is no object. But what are you going to do about that jalapeño field? Stupid you. You signed without reading the fine print. Do you own the land? Another payment to make on top of the two hundred Ks? Will you have to deal with some hostile farmer backed by crooked lawyers?"*

MEETING CONSUELO – Nov 15, 2013

By the front door, a dark-skinned ageless looking lady is proudly sitting in a tall rattan wingchair. Wearing a neat colorful long dress, her presence gives an unmistakable message: "*Here I am. The boss*." Yet her assertive stance is tempered by and whimsical eyes shining in her deeply wrinkled face.

"Señora Consuelo," intones the agent, "if I may, I'd like to have the honor to introduce Señora Vasquez, the new owner. Señora Vasquez this is Consuelo, your hotel manager."

"I already know Señora Consuelo well," jokes Rosa with a bitter smile.

Consuelo's face beams with pride after hearing what she thinks is a compliment. She gets up from her chair and says "I know you too. I knew you even before you arrived. Come, come, Señora Vasquez, let me hug you."

Rosa lets herself be taken on her new employee's ample bosom. But she feels embarrassed, realizing that Consuelo's enthusiasm was triggered by a fake compliment that was in fact an underhanded sarcasm.

Taken back, Consuelo, sensing the hesitation of her new owner, asks anxiously "How did you get here from San Diego"?

"By plane," answers Rosa, without noticing the worried look of Consuelo.

"Ouch, the plane is no good for women!"

Rosa does not know what to say.

The agent takes advantage of the short lull with a new push "*Muy bien*. Now that you and Señora Consuelo get along, I have to explain something else. It's about the jalapeño field. Two acres. A good deal, no? A farmer rents it from you. But he keeps farming it, forever."

"What? Again?" shouts Rosa.

Ignoring the interruption, Señor Gimenez goes on "Sorry. It's in the contract you signed, Señora Vasquez. The farmer, he gives you ten percent of the crop each year. Good, no?"

Consuelo confirms "Yeah! Each year. 2,000 pesos. Almost a whole hundred dollars!"

His theatrical act over, the agent makes a point to fade away before Rosa has a chance to ask any more questions.

"Facebook did not say anything about Jalapeños, either" silently mopes Rosa. She is baffled by this new dishonest trick. *"Well, Rosa dear, at least the acreage is not too bad. You can turn that field into a fancy garden. But how to get rid of a legally protected immovable renter, in a country you know nothing about?"*

⚜

The initial contact went rather well. Rosa and Consuelo sized each other up. They realize that despite their age and cultural differences, their personalities are complementary. But the competitive instinct takes over. There can only be one 'boss'. Somewhat unwillingly, they slip into a kind of comical verbal match.

Rosa tries to find a way to start the conversation while carefully hiding her inner thoughts. Consuelo, as the official hotel manager, takes the initiative with a vigorous "Señora Vasquez …"

On her side, feeling instinctively the need to assert herself on the spot, Rosa-the-hotel owner, launches a banter to her employee in a tone that tries to be imposing "Señora Consuelo, from now on, please call me Rosa."

Consuelo's deeply wrinkled face turns into a sly smile. "Señora Vasquez, from now on, please call me Consuelo."

Consuelo had the last word. She is the one who will be the 'boss'.

A residue of underlying tension lingers, but both Rosa and Consuelo know that they have given birth to a lasting friendship.

MOVING IN THE OLD LA LINDA – Nov 15, 2013

Consuelo clears her throat, sits up in her rattan chair and starts her official welcome speech "*Muy bien*. Let me take you in and show you around, Rosa. Before that, let me tell you something important. Two weeks ago, right before El Dia de Muertos, the agent told me that a young lady from San Diego was going to be the new owner. That's too bad you did not come at the time of El Dia de Muertos. You would have enjoyed it. El Dia de Muertos is beautiful here. It is very important for you to understand the meaning of the Day of the Dead, if you want to be a good hotel owner. You'll see it next year, God willing."

"Yes!" Rosa jumps on the opportunity to say something positive, as she thinks "*Rosa dear, it is true that this lady Consuelo was not mentioned in the Facebook ad. But she seems to be a pretty nice person. The real estate guy was right. She might very well be the key to La Linda's business success. An ally … or a thorn in your thigh …Depending on your attitude … No anger … Show appreciation and respect … Consuelo has to be the manager. That's an OK arrangement. You could not do anything by yourself, anyway. This way, you Rosa dear, will have time to focus on your research … and your own healing.*"

"You know," continues Consuelo "I was scared that maybe you were a Gringo woman. No good, right? Then the agent told me your name was Vasquez. So, I told him if her name is Vasquez, it's OK to sell the hotel to her. And not someone else, you know what I mean? That is why you are here, Rosa. Thanks to me. We do not want no Gringo owner here, right? "

"I see," answers Rosa to be polite. But right away she figures: "*Do you see Consuelo's point? She is the one who approved you! You must therefore approve her. Plain and simple. She is the boss. Without Consuelo's OK, you would not even be here, Rosa dear.*"

Consuelo goes on, "You make me happy. Because your name is Vasquez, it means that you are one of us, Señora. After I made sure that you were one of us and not a Gringo woman, my daughter Carmensita and I fixed your bedroom. Just so. My son Juanito was a carpenter, you know. Very strong.

He built a new bed, a new armoire with a mirror he found in Los Cabos flea market and a new bookcase. He got two mirrors. He gave you the best one. Just for you. Don Pedro has blessed the mirror. So, you do not have to worry about anything."

"*The mirror was blessed*?" ponders Rosa. She wants to be diplomatic. After the real-estate agent's weird comments, she realizes that this superstition, while new to her, might just the tip of an iceberg of entangled beliefs that seem to interfere with all business decisions and deals.

"Oh, I am not worried, Consuelo. You know what's the right thing to do, for sure."

⚘

Emboldened by Rosa's approval, Consuelo pursues: "As you know, it is bad luck to use the furniture of dead people who have not been buried."

"Yes, I know that," lies Rosa nervously, to hide that faint but weird electric shock that has just invaded her, head to toe.

Rosa's bizarre jerk startles Consuelo. She swiftly changes the subject.

"You can pay my son 4,000 pesos. Whenever you want."

"I will do that," says Rosa while thinking: "*I am willing to accept the superstitions. But what is that new twist of dead people who have not been buried? Is that what the real estate guy was muttering about? Is that why local people did not want to buy the property? Fishy. A bit scary, too. But that's OK. We'll deal with whatever comes along, as needed. I'd like to know about that Don Pedro, though.*"

⚘

In a flash, Rosa realizes that she is entering a new universe. Baja is different from the worlds she has known. Europe, Africa and the US.

She feels confused. As if falling into a 'time warp' of her own making. The fear-driven notions she fabricated while in San Diego are now confronted by reality. She feels strangely enmeshed by concentric cocoons of whitish,

15

gooey veils. A new PTSD panic attack starts creeping up her spine. For no apparent reason. She stops talking to Consuelo and goes into an internal monologue.

"Rosa dear, you are not in that terrible place anymore. The place where fear invaded your whole being, your spirit, your soul. The San Diego shrink said that you should settle in a new place. That is where you are now, Rosa dear. There are new realities to face, of course. You are entering in a new society. You must. You can. You will do it!"

To control the attack, she asks for a glass of water. "Thank you, Consuelo."

She is surprised to notice the tenderness of her own voice. This is a welcome improvement. Often, in personal conversations, since her PTSD started, she could only talk in mechanical tones. Meanwhile she goes on with her soothing inner monologue.

"Let's face it, running to the end of the world is not a solution. Matter of fact, Rosa dear, there is no such thing as the 'end of the world'. To heal, you will have to become one, among your new hosts. To earn their support, you must be honest. Within yourself. With them."

Bam! The fear vanishes, replaced with dark rambling self-talk.

"But be careful, though. Harsh honesty might drive them away. Will you dare give up your Western logic-based mentality? Will you survive without the intellectual rationalism and all the constructs that created your superego? On the other hand, your new hosts have preserved a zone where spirituality still prevails. For them, creative mysticism seems to blend with their daily affairs in a seamless continuity. Like primal foundations and driving forces. Could Consuelo and her kin possess truths that you, and all your western cohorts, cannot even comprehend? Will you be able to merge those two opposite worldviews? Remember that you already have a shattered self. Will you have to go on wearing a mask to hide your insecurities? Or will you be able to explore human commonalities … and enjoy Life, again?"

Consuelo is baffled to see this otherwise pleasant middle-aged woman who stands still in front of her, glaring eyes wide-open, in a silent daze.

"Esta nueva dueña es loca!"

[This new owner is crazy!]," she mutters.

Rosa realizes that she has briefly lost contact with reality. Her mind has been floating around. With a strong conscious effort, she snaps herself away from the anxious cogitations. She feels the unconscious need to shake her head for an unknown reason. Was it a trance? Did it last one minute … or ten minutes … or maybe longer? *"Rosa dear, you must bring herself back together. Stop rocking your crazy head. To protect your self … otherwise you will fall back into the obsessive pit … Never, never, never again!"*

Suddenly she stops her inner rambling.

The internal monologue returns.

"Assert yourself, Rosa dear. Remember. You have decided to be a no-nonsense businesswoman. You just made a significant investment. Do not stand there silent as a mummy. Talk! Just say something. Does not matter what."

To end an embarrassing silence, Rosa goes on: "Hey, Consuelo, please tell me about the jalapeños, will you? Who takes care of the jalapeños? Can I turn the farm into a garden?"

Consuelo inhales a big gulp of air, shouting in a sudden rage.

"Dios mío, absolutamente no."

"You scared me, lady! First, you stopped talking for a long time, your eyes wide open. And then you shake your head like a goat gone crazy for eating coca leaves! And then you come up with your jalapeño story? What's the matter with you? Tell me! Do you have bad spirits inside you? Do not talk to me about the jalapeños, you hear me, kid? Never!"

After a pause to regain her composure, Consuelo switches to a motherly but firm tone: "You must be tired from the trip. That's why you act funny. Or maybe it is the change of air. Or maybe your trip on the plane was no good. Bad spirits on the plane, up there, you know. Plane is no good, I tell you. The sky is for birds. Not for people. Bad luck. Look, because I like you, I will ask Don Pedro what's best about the jalapeños. He will decide. But do not say nothing about the jalapeños. Never. You hear me, girl?"

Rosa is surprised by Consuelo's sharp reaction about what should be a small business matter. She is puzzled, annoyed. And that Don Pedro's comes up too often during each important business conversation. *"It's my business, damn it!"* She'd like to say something. Instead, she forces herself to keep quiet. Bitter and ashamed for not being able to say anything.

After that snappy interaction, Consuelo feels totally in charge.

She has won Round One of the Consuelo vs. Rosa contest.

Consuelo figures that she can now reduce the pressure on this new almost-Gringo owner who is not so bad. She chooses to switch back to her sweet self. With a friendly but condescending tone, she goes on: "Come on, Señora Vasquez. It's so nice to finally know you. Let me show you the upstairs. Be careful, the top step is broken. As long as you know which one is broken, that's OK, no?"

A lanky boy had taken position on one of the living room chairs.

"Hey, you there," commands Consuelo. "Take the lady's suitcases upstairs. Better be careful."

They reach the small upstairs landing. Beaming, Consuelo opens the bedroom door, with a majestic gesture. "Here you are, just for you …"

Rosa enjoys the sincere welcome. All of this is new for her. She never experienced the sweetness of family life. Consuelo's motherly mannerism is a little overdone. But Rosa welcomes the simple interaction. She feels appreciated, valued, just as she is. "Thank you, Consuelo. I love this bedroom. I like the Mexican colonial antique look of the furniture. Your son is quite talented. Does he have a business of his own?"

FIB NUMBER TWO – Nov 15, 2013

"No, Rosa, he now works at the fish market. More money," answers Consuelo as she gestures to the padded rattan bedroom chairs. "Let's sit down. It's better to sit … Well, to continue. Carpentry is his hobby. Juanito is a good son. My other son Alessandro is dead. (She crosses herself three times). He used to be good, too. But the drug gang thing, you know. The *Federales*, you know, they shoot him. Juanito is strong, as I told you. No drugs. He has five children of his own. Rosa, do you have children and grandchildren? And where are they?"

"*Here she is again*," mutters Rosa to herself, before going on with "Well, Consuelo. I do not have any children."

Over the years, many people have asked Rosa the same question. She has trained herself to casually give a soft negative answer. As a childless middle-aged woman, the question revives her secret pain. Deep inside her soul. Now permanent. Like an open wound.

—————

Consuelo is intrigued and annoyed by Rosa's evasive response. She is determined to resume her pointed interrogation. "So, you do not have any children. And Señor Gimenez he told me you forgot where you are from? Tell me, Rosa. You are not from Baja, for sure, hahaha! And, based on your lovely accent and the clever words you use, you are not from Mexico City, either …"

Rosa did not expect to be grilled so soon and with such intensity while taking possession of a $200,000 ramshackle hotel. "I am from very far away, Consuelo," she says in dodging despair, while trying to figure some satisfactory answer.

"Where is that 'very far' you talk about, child?" Consuelo does not like vague statements, you see.

In a jiffy, Rosa concocts a clever fib. The best answer will have to cover both her fake ethnicity and her real Spanish accent. "Dear Consuelo, I am a Wichi. Where I come from, we are *Indios*, Native Americans from Argentina.

I was born in the town of Orán. You know, Northwest of Argentina. In the mountains near Chili."

Consuelo could not care less about South America's geography. She proceeds with her interrogation: "*Muy bien*. And now why do you talk so well like you do, if you are just an *India*? That does not make no sense."

Rosa's brain goes into its fastest spin ever. "I was an orphan, Consuelo. Left on the steps of the church. The nuns in Orán raised me. They sent me to catholic school and then to the university. You know, we people in Argentina, we speak Castilian Spanish ..."

"*Muy bien*!" Now, this is what I call a good answer. So, you are an Argentinian *mestiza*? That's good! Now I understand! Here, we are all *mestizos*! *Muy bien*!"

Consuelo is all tickled for having forced Rosa to share what was obviously a personal secret ...

Rosa, on her side, is pleased to have so rapidly concocted a clever fib that will stick, for sure.

Round Two of the Consuelo-Rosa bout is a tie. Time for a break.

"Yes, that is what I am. A *mestiza* from Argentina," says Rosa, in an attempt to put an end to the intrusive conversation.

"*Muy bien*. We will call you La Inca," gloats Consuelo, unfazed.

"No, not Inca! We, Wichis, do not like no Incas," emphasizes Rosa with the utmost sincerity. She feels relieved. Her fib seems to have confused and, as a result, quelled down Consuelo's inquisitive mind ... for now, at least.

But she suddenly realizes the enormity of the mistake she just made. She has been In Todos Santos for only two hours. And yet, she has already concocted two conflicting lies about her identity.

The real estate agent knows her as a Spaniard. And now Consuelo believes that she is an Argentinian from Native American origin. "*That's OK, Rosa dear. There are more critical issues to tackle. But from this point on, stick to the Native American image. It will fit well. And Consuelo is probably more respected in town than the real estate agent – who must be despised by most common folks."*

Consuelo looks pensive, closing her eyes, while saying: "Good. Yes, I remember. Just after I got married, long time ago, some tourists from Argentina came to Baja. They stayed here at La Linda. When it was nice here, you know. Not like now with all the troubles because of the spirits. You are right. You are talking just like them Argentinians. Welcome to Baja California, Argentina lady! You will like it here, for sure. People are friendly here. They will love you, too! You are one of us, really …"

TAKING POSSESSION OF LA LINDA – Nov 15, 2013

Evening arrives.

After multiple tours of the ruined hotel and its surroundings, followed by a growing number of neighborhood kids gawking at her, Rosa is at last back in her bedroom.

Laying in her new bed, she reflects on her first day's achievements, before starting her meditation and her internal dialog.

So much has happened during this first day in Baja. *"Your $200,000 hotel of yours is not fit for legal habitation. But at least, Rosa dear, you have a really comfortable bed! And you are welcome by a bunch of lovely people … something that you never experienced before … wherever else you might have been."*

She learned how to meditate from her San Diego University therapist. It helps her. Sometimes. To control and quash down her obsessive fears and nightmare-ridden nights. Tonight, the meditation does the job.

"Rosa. Rosa dear. Relax. You now own a hotel in Todos Santos … In Baja, right at the end of the world, where you wanted to be … Lost in the local crowds … Those kids were so cute! Consuelo will manage the place. She loves that. And you, Rosa dear, you will only have to take it easy, I guess. Thanks to Consuelo's friendly gossip around town, you will always be welcomed as an Argentinian … But nobody in Todos Santos must ever know where you came from … Block those damned fears … For sure you will remain totally unknown … Well done, Rosa dear … All is going according to plan … as of now …"

Whack! Harsh reality rushes back. *"Hey, you idiot! You are nice and cosy in this cute bedroom, right? As you ran away from San Diego's safety, did you ever think where you would spend the night? Where would you be if it were not for Consuelo's friendly machinations? You arrived here unprepared, Rosa dear, like a runaway kid. You had not even figured where you were going to spend your first night."*

—⸻∽⁓∿⁓∽⸻—

The soothing song she sometimes hates comes back in her head before fading away.

> *'What a lovely place … What a lovely face.'*

—⸻∽⁓∿⁓∽⸻—

Relaxed, she slowly drifts away into a deep sleep.

Morning arrives, soft as a white feather floating down in the still air.

After carefully skipping the broken step, she arrives in the musty-smelling downstairs. The breakfast is already served on the dining room table. Her large ceramic plate is loaded with scrambled eggs, beans, tortillas. The works. Next to it (you guessed right) is a generous bowl of deep-fried jalapeños.

Sitting on a chair next to an imposing armoire, Consuelo seems to be dozing. Or is she just resting? Or muttering a morning prayer?

"*Buenos dias*, **Rosa**."

"*Buenos dias*, **Señora Consuelo**."

"*Me llama Consuelo solamente, para ti*." **[For you, my name is just Consuelo]**

'Le deseo un buen día, Consuelo…'

"**First, enjoy your breakfast, Rosa. I fixed** *machaca*. **Just for you.**" Then to start the day, the most important thing is to show you the *ofrenda*. You will like it. It is for us. For the La Linda hotel. For all the guests. I have setup it up in the drawing room. Five years ago. Come with me, child."

"**I am following you,**" says Rosa.

"**Sorry. I forgot that you are Argentinian and not Mexican. Maybe in Argentina you do not say** *ofrenda*. **It can be called an altar, too. We call it** *ofrenda* **because it is there to offer gifts to the dead, you know.**"

"**Thanks for telling me.**"

23

THE OFRENDA – Nov 16, 2013

Nail heads are poking out of the termite-chewed floor. But the western wall, with its tiny window facing the ocean, has been given a fresh coat of white paint. Surrounded by chairs set against the walls, a wooden triangular altar is covered with cloth of vivid colors. All kinds of daily life objects, marigold flowers and lit candles are placed around the faded photo of a man and his wife in their fifties. In answer to Rosa's silent question, Consuelo explains: "this is our *ofrenda*. Small. But just what Señor and Señora Gomez want."

Moved by Consuelo's sincere fervor, Rosa feels embarrassed for only giving a bland comment, worthy of a would-be tourist. "It's very interesting!"

Consuelo launches an elaborate explanation "As I said before, this altar is not very big. I would even say that it is small. But it does have three floors. One for Heaven. Another one for the Earth. And the third for the dead. Other altars have seven floors.

"Why seven floors?" asks Rosa, just to show her interest.

"It is for each of the stages that the deceased must go through before reaching Paradise," Consuelo explains in a low voice.

On the right, mounted on a large blue plate, is a ceramic figurine of a fishing boat, wrecked and laying on its side. On the left, a bunch of statuettes stand without any apparent order: colorful ceramic fish and imaginary sea creatures of varied sizes, a little mound of ceramic jalapeños, gnomes, buns, figurines of the Virgin Mary, a tragically painful Christ bleeding on his cross, a hanging rosary and other religious objects.

"You see, Rosa, maybe you people in Argentina do not do anything like this."

"Oh, yes, Consuelo, we Wichi people, we have a great love and respect for our dead."

"That is good, Rosita. But here, we have extra respect. You see? Those are the pictures of Señor Gonzales and his dear wife Manuela; may God bless their souls. And here, as you can see, is their fishing boat. Capsized."

Rosa is moved by Consuelo's quivering voice and the tender spirituality she expresses about the dead couple. She tries to bond with Consuelo's mystical experience. Or at least empathize with her. But, in a quick pang of painful consciousness, she realizes that she has never experienced such personal feelings about dead people. Except for her dad. But that was different.

"They seemed to be such nice people," says Rosa. She immediately feels embarrassed by the platitude of her comment.

"Oh, yes, Rosa. Nice people, but poor. No money from the hotel. Only from the jalapeño farm. I do the hotel. For poor people who don't have no money, the hoboes, you know. They do the jalapeños. Every day in the early morning they go fishing. To sell fish to the restaurants, you know. One day a big wave came from nowhere."

"Oh, you mean a tsunami, a tidal wave? I read that tsunamis happen quite often here in Baja."

"What are you saying, girl? No, you don't understand. And don't you ever repeat that, you hear me? After Señor and Señora Gomez died, a big big wave spilled over all the beaches at the same time. The sea covered the beach and all the jalapeños. Ripped them off their roots. And the sea comes right here inside the hotel. Way high. And then the wood becomes rotten. We call it *maremotto*. Don Pedro, he knows. He is our *curandero*. He says *maremotto* is from the spirits of people who died in the sea. You know, Don Pedro is our *curandero*. Gringo people they call him shaman. No. He is *curandero*."

She crosses herself while closing her eyes. "We do not want the *maremotto* to come back. Right? We must make the departed happy. You understand, girl? The *maremotto* covered the hotel almost to the roof. And because of the salt, the jalapeños they grow small.

"I see," says Rosa. She does not want to bother Consuelo's grieving nor counterdict her spiritual beliefs.

"Now, Rosa, I must tell you something. Now you are the one who owns the hotel. This means that the *ofrenda* is yours. I take care of it. But it is your *ofrenda*. Do you have pictures of your mom and your dad? Put them right here, under Señor and Señora Gomez's photo. This way Nuestra Señora de Guadalupe will protect them and all of us at the same time!" continues

25

Consuelo while signing herself at each critical steps of her complex theological explanation. "You do not want the bad spirits to cast the evil eye on your hotel and everybody in it, do you?"

While talking, in measured steps, Consuelo respectfully approaches the altar. She ever so slightly re-arranges the shipwreck display, piously choosing what she considers to be a more realistic angle.

Rosa follows every move, every gesture, intent on absorbing Consuelo's state of mind, while trying to figure how to give a credible explanation to the thorny issue about her own parents.

FIB NUMBER THREE – Nov 16, 2013

"Well, Consuelo. Putting my parents' pictures would be the right thing to do. But what you say makes me sad. As I told you I was left as an orphan on the steps of the nuns' convent in Orán. So, you see, I do not have pictures of my poor parents. They gave me up. They were too poor to feed me."

Rosa feels ashamed for fabricating such an outrageous lie while Consuelo is expressing profoundly sincere feelings. Yet her top priority is to cover her pains. To cut from the past. To protect herself from future pains. At any cost.

"Is that the real truth, child?" Consuelo has noticed some hesitation in Rosa's phony confession. "You told me that you were abandoned. I might believe that. But before, you told me that you were abandoned on the church steps. And now you tell me it was on the orphanage steps."

"Yes. It is absolutely true." Caught, Rosa cannot hide her defensive tone. She only manages to hide her lie with a geographically correct fact: "Orán is a town in Northwest Argentina. Next to the Chile mountains."

"That's all right. That's all right. You've already told me that, girl. If you do not have pictures, you can write little cards saying 'Rosa's daddy' and 'Rosa's mommy'. Write neatly. Because even if you do not know your father. Even if you do not know your mother. Even if they gave you up as a baby. They are still your parents. They love you. You love them. Their picture on the *ofrenda* makes them happy. Makes them proud of you. And help them in their after-life travels to heaven."

⫸⫷⫸⫷⫸

With a pinch in her heart, Rosa ponders "Dear Rosa, *Consuelo expresses it so well when she says 'Make them proud of you'. You just discovered a big void in your miserable life.*"

"Thank you, Consuelo. These are thoughtful suggestions. Please give me the cards. I will write the names." Her voice is quivering. Surprised, she finds herself barely able to hold her tears. She realizes that she has not shed tears for years. Anguished, she mutters "Daddy?" before tightening her lips into a pitiful grimace she cannot hide.

⸺⟨∘⟩⟨∘⟩⟨∘⟩⸺

Consuelo stands up slowly. Takes a few steps. Tenderly holds Rosa on her ample bosom.

"I am happy for you, Rosa. Cry for your dear parents. Crying is good for the dead. Your crying makes them happy. They are with you. Right here in this room when you cry like this. These are tears of joy, Rosa."

Overwhelmed by the depth of Consuelo's religious mysticism, Rosa's instinctive rationality collapses like a house of cards.

A balm of peace invades her.

Consuelo's tone of voice soon flips from motherly to severely inquisitive. "But let me tell you something important, child. You can lie to me ... or to anybody else ... that does not matter too much ... everybody lies to everybody else, right? ... Maybe I believe you. Maybe Don Pedro believes you. Just to be nice, you know ... But do not ever lie to the spirits ... Do you hear me, girl? You do not want the spirits to seek revenge, do you?"

Rosa tries to hide her embarrassment with a weak, childlike smile. Meanwhile, waves of guilt invade her consciousness *"Rosa dear, how can you spin those fibs, intertwined with fake emotions, when Consuelo and all the people around her are so sincere and so giving of themselves?"*

Yet, in an uncontrolled reaction, she spins another lie. To mend the awkward mystical situation, she goes on a devious offensive with an absurd poke of her own. "Consuelo, I have an idea. I could add the name of Sister Carmen. She is the nun who was so good to me at the orphanage, 'member? That would be nice, no?"

"Perhaps ... I mean yes," says Consuelo. "Here are small white paper cards that Carlos gave me the other day." There still is a hint of suspicion in her voice as she squints her eyes, trying to decode Rosa's facial expression.

This time, Consuelo is not sure.

She reluctantly admits that Rosa has won Round Three.

While writing three cards labelled 'Pappi', 'Mama' and 'Hermana Carmen', Rosa launches another half-fib half-truth story. As a strategic diversion she expands "You see, Consuelo, Sister Carmen taught me how to read and write. Then she helped me through school. She passed, may God bless her soul, when I was a student at Buenos Aires University. Thanks to her, I now am a professor of archaeology."

—◁/◁/◁—

Taking advantage of Consuelo's temporary confusion, she launches a quick spin. "Did I tell you that I want to go visit the Baja cave rock paintings? ...."

The red herring question does the job. Consuelo's enthusiasm resurfaces as she straightens up. "Oh yes, the cave paintings! Yes, I know. Carlos told me about those things up north. I never saw that. He did. Our priest at church, he says to not look. Bad luck, you know. Carlos is the mail carrier. When he was young, he was making money by taking tourists to the caves. Crazy Gringo scientists go there. I don't know why. They go over the mountains, you know. Difficult to walk. They crazy, I tell you. And now Carlos still studies a lot about Mexican *Indios* at the Public Library. He says he is one of the last from the Guaycura people. He even wants to write a book, he says. Rosa, when you ever receive mail from anybody or anywhere, Carlos will come here to deliver the mail. And then you will meet him ... because he is the mail carrier, as I told you ..."

Consuelo's non-stop hints of mistrust are getting on Rosa's nerves. This time around, instead of figuring out some other dodging response, Rosa decides to play possum: "Well, Consuelo, in that case, just ask him to visit us ... Even if there is no mail ... It will be a pleasure."

FIB NUMBER THREE AND A HALF – Nov 16, 2013

A new pang of anxiety invades Rosa *"Mail? Me, receiving mail here? I never thought about that,"* she ponders. *"Nobody is supposed to know who I am nor where I am. Therefore, I will never receive any mail here. All my mail goes to San Diego U. and will pile up there. I must now prove that I am Argentinian. As soon as possible, once there is Internet service at the hotel, I will go on-line to order magazines from the Buenos Aires Scientific Society. If it takes too much time to get the Internet, I'll do it from the Public Library. I will add Argentinian scientists to my Facebook 'friends' and correspond with them by regular mail. That way, people here will conclude that I really am Argentinian. Consuelo's suspicions will stop for good. You just made a bright move, Rosa dear."*

MEETING CARLOS – Dec 7, 2013

As the days go by, eager-beaver Consuelo hopes to see some mail arrive for Rosa. Does not matter where the mail comes from. As long as it arrives in Todos Santos, addressed to this somehow mysterious new owner.

No correo. Nada.

[No mail. Nothing].

But Consuelo can do better than just wait, right? Do not worry. She'll find some other way. She has many tricks up her sleeve.

That is how, in the absence of any mail for Rosa, on the third Saturday, at exactly eleven thirty, Carlos pops up, supposedly unannounced, for a courtesy visit to Hotel La Linda. It just happens that Consuelo has prepared a tête-à-tête lunch table, with candles and all.

In his best white suit, Carlos takes off his fine panama hat, uncovering a braid of deeply black hair that matches his dark copper tone skin. Flowers in one hand and a thick manuscript in the other, he politely submits to Consuelo's ceremonial introduction routine.

"Rosa, this is Carlos Romero. He is our letter carrier."

Right away, Carlos takes over with a respectful "It is a real honor to meet you, Doctor Vasquez … "

"She likes to be called Rosa," interrupts Consuelo before going on in the same breath: "and, you know, Rosa, I must tell you that Carlos is not married. Not even engaged to any girl. The last one, she died, may Santa Maria bless her soul." Consuelo signs herself out of respect for Carlos' previous *novia*.

Consuelo adjusts herself in the high-back rattan chair next to the altar, proud of her achievement. Everything Is going well. These two will get together, God willing. She loves playing the matchmaker game, you know. In fact, it's one of her jobs in town. People even say that half of the babies in Todos Santos arrived in this world thanks to her magical interventions!

Carlos ignores Consuelo's obvious matchmaking antics. She has tried to practice those tricks on him before. The last time was with a divorcee with four kids. Like everyone in town, he respects Consuelo. But, beware, he is his own man. "Doctor Vasquez, I hear that you are planning to visit the cave murals at Mulegé in the Sierra de San Francisco. Beautiful work done there during the period of the Yumano culture. I'd like to know how long ago. Not sufficiently studied in the professional literature. The people who painted those rocks deserve recognition. You'll see. It is 350 miles from here."

"That far? I thought it was just around here …"

"Oh, no. It is in El Norte region. It takes more than eight hours to drive there. Through La Paz, you know. On the other side, I tell you. Mulegé is a beautiful oasis. So green. That is where my ancestors were living, before they were pushed south to the desertic area where we are, by new Native Americans from the north. It has a wide river and many trees. Not at all like our deserts around here, for sure! I've been there many times. That is how I became crazy."

"You do not seem to be crazy, Carlos."

"Well, thank you for your thoughtful opinion, Doctor Vasquez," says Carlos with a whimsical smile. "But some people in Todos Santos think otherwise! It is believed that when people look at the paintings for too long, their soul gets shredded out of their skull. Those are false ideas spread by the Spanish Jesuits. What Is true is that these paintings invite us to pause and reflect. They take the viewer to another world. One can even go into out-of-body experiences by sharing feelings with the impassioned individuals who create those art pieces thousands of years ago. Whatever the reason might be, that is the way I became an apprentice archaeologist. Around here, we, native groups who managed to survive, are proud of our own identity."

"What you say is profound on a human level and touching on a personal level, Carlos," says Rosa. "I often had the same feelings of communion across the ages. What you are saying is truly remarkable. Moreover, your experience is unique. Because you integrate your filial respect for your ancestors while validating them from a scientific point of view, according to a process that you yourself have developed."

"Again, I thank you for your kind comments, Dr. Vasquez. In conclusion, we, true indigenous people, are trying to manage our survival. In a hostile social environment, although we are in our ancestral lands. We draw our strength from the respect of our own identity, despised by our successive invaders.

The end result was cultural erosion and eventual annihilation. Which proves, unfortunately, that 'Might makes right'. We come from many isolated tribes that existed along the peninsula. The Paipais, the Kiliwas and my Guaycuras. We had distinctive characteristics, habits, languages and beliefs. But we also had many similarities because intermarriage between tribes was very frequent. Made of the same human substance, you understand? Now we are a disappearing minority. Most of the people here are not true natives. They are converted mestizos who emigrated from mainland Mexico. Imported en masse in the nineteenth century to work in semi-slavery in the sugar cane fields ... and later abandoned because of several years of drought, part of a general climate change. Nobody wants to hear what happened here when Spain invaded our lands. And especially not what happened to my Guaycura ancestors."

Rosa is amazed by the depth and the painful intimacy of Carlos' analysis. "You are giving me a very significant historical shortcut, Carlos. You describe with ease and veracity facts and feelings that I have never been able to express, in spite of - probably because of - my scientific work."

"For me, it is simple, concludes Carlos. First I want to know. Then I want other people to know. Maybe I am crazy. I just want the world to know about my ancestors and how they were ruthlessly decimated."

At that moment, Consuelo-the-matchmaker wakes up from her feigned nap *"Muy bien*, young people. I am happy that you had a good time. I did not understand your scientific gibberish. One hour is enough for today."

"Alright, Consuelo," says Carlos.

"Alright, Consuelo," echoes Rosa.

"Carlos, you can come back next Saturday. At the same time."

"Thank you, Consuelo. And goodbye, Doctor Vasquez."

That night, as she slips between her sheets after her prescribed meditation, Rosa cannot stop herself from thinking about Carlos: *"Such a good-looking man! He is really in remarkable shape. Nice male profile too! His gestures are so fluid. I like that braided hair of his. And those long muscles under his smooth, evenly copper colored skin ..."* She catches herself breathing hard.

33

"Come on, Rosa dear. Come on, for Pete's sake, slow down what's left of your hormones. You are fifty-two, remember? And he called you Professor Vasquez. Cool down, Rosa. Cool down, I said. The way he looks, he could almost be one of your students ..."

Students ...

Students ...

The word 'students' triggers a shudder down her spine. She barely manages to prevent a new episode.

But the memory of Carlos's virile charm soon helps her fall into a blissful sleep.

PATCHING THE OLD WRECK –
Dec 2013 to May 2014

From December 2013 to May 2014, the renovation work started slowly … only to proceed even more slowly after stopping for Christmas. And then temperatures climbed up more than usual, as the days went by.

Nobody wants to do construction work when the temp is in the upper eighties, right?

Despite it all, just to be nice, Carlos, Juanito and neighborhood teenagers have offered to work on week-end mornings. At their own pace. Using recycled lumber and scarce supplies to stay within budget and according to local building traditions. Colorful adobe bricks slapped on cheap cement blocks create that unmistakably Todos Santos architectural flair.

Consuelo supervises. She cannot contain her enthusiasm. Each incremental improvement is cause for mini-celebrations

"¡Esta puerta es tan hermosa! … ¡Que linda ventana!"

[This door is so beautiful! … What a cute window!]

Rosa has been assigned to kitchen duty, working with Consuelo's daughter. Learning the Baja recipes has a soul-healing effect that Rosa never experienced before. She is frustrated for being put on the side-line. Owner of an expensive ruin under amateurish renovations, she has been reduced to silence. She is frustrated to know that each new door, each new window that Consuelo raves about will last only a few months, at best.

"On the other hand. Rosa dear, do your kitchen work. It is important for several reasons. Do not gripe, complain or feel sorry for yourself. Forget about big jobs and ego-boosting responsibilities. The stress of your old job nearly killed you. This is a good period for you to immerse yourself in this almost magical world. Discover its hidden riches. Love and be loved by its easy-going people. Take a long, long break. You need it."

⟞⟨⟩⟨⟩⟨⟩⟝

Consuelo has no interest whatsoever about the solidity or longevity of the refurbished 'La Linda'. Asserting her life-long position as hotel manager, she has already started a word-of-mouth advertising campaign among the locals. Extending her matchmaker contacts, she offers one-week discounts to all new couples who met and courted through her services. Enchanted local newlyweds rent rooms, ignoring that the hotel is still undergoing major repairs … Some paying guests even give a hand in their 'spare time', inspired by Consuelo's mystical aura.

PROFOUND CONVERSATIONS – Dec 2013 to May 2014

Months go by as the patching jobs eek along.

Every so often, Rosa and Carlos have casual contacts for trivial construction-related issues.

Less and less self-conscious, they plan and enjoy weekend or evening chats.

Yet Carlos, aware of Consuelo's protocols, makes a point to ask for her permission to meet his 'date'. He feels like a little schoolboy for having to do that. But he knows that the embarrassment is worth it.

Rosa, on the other hand, is secretly amused by those little immature games that she never experienced in her youth.

On one such Saturday afternoon, over coffees served by Consuelo, the two return to their freewheeling conversations.

"Can I finish the discussion we had the other day? The topic means a lot to me. And you are the first person who gave me a sincere support."

"Of course. Go ahead, Carlos. What you already told me was exciting."

"The Baja indigenous people were attacked and massacred by Cortez and his successors during two whole centuries. The Spaniards were intent on setting up colonies and missions. The local tribes were not united. Yet they fought back valiantly. Those were the most asymmetrical battles in the humanity's history. The natives were still at the stone age level. Their most lethal weapons were silex arrow heads! The invaders were hardened military fighters with ships, horses, armors, swords, axes and whatever weapons were in vogue in already war-crazy Europe."

"Good analysis, Carlos. I have read of similar conflicts fought elsewhere during colonial times in North Africa. You are right, the military disparity here in Baja was never surpassed."

"Thank you. The trouble is that the end result was systematic genocides, physical enslavement, cultural eradication, followed by the spread of diseases, systematic neglect and rejection into abject poverty. Nowadays, those actions fall under the label of crimes against humanity. Yet the perpetrators, from Columbus to Cortez and beyond, are glorified in our children's schoolbooks."

After a long pause, Carlos goes on "You see, Professor. That is why, whenever I am not on my mail route, I go to the Public Library. Doing research or writing about those crimes against my ancestors, you know. Ancestors who had created a particular way of life that has now disappeared. A way of life that was as valid as any other one. I used to be upset. Studying has reduced my bitterness. I realize that other tribes, other nations have been exterminated, too. Military domination, killings, war, terrorism are all manifestations of a human mental derangement. Spain had its Cortez. Germany had its Hitler."

"Yes, and France had its colonial war generals," shares Rosa. "That's interesting and sad, Carlos. So, that is the way you got the archaeology bug? Motivated by your passion for your vanished ancestors?"

"I like your expression. Yes, I got the bug as a guide for UCLA PhD students of Professor Hohenthal. You know, going on mountain trails. Or visiting local *Indios*, interpreting and what not. They gave me the title of 'consultant'. And gave me good money. That's the way I was able to buy my first ethnology books! That was before I became a letter-carrier. I got that job because I could read the envelopes and could walk many miles around town. I learned a whole lot more since then. For my job, I walk around all the time around Todos Santos. Walking has kept me in shape. At least my legs. Walking is good for the soul, I tell you. For me, I figure that I inherited that walking and running capacity from my ancestors. It's in my DNA, no doubt. Hunter gatherers, they were perpetually on the move, from the mountains to the shore and back, according to the seasons and the available resources. Imagine that. For millenaries! Fish and salt from the ocean. Pinions and rabbits from the land. Those are the survival habits that Professor Hohenthal described so accurately. The life I would like to live, if I only could."

—*∂/∂/∂*—

"So, you are familiar with the monumental work that Professor Hohenthal has done?"

"I read them all! They are instructive but not enough is said about this southern part of Baja. At the beginning, I had to study a lot just to be able to read professional literature. Word by word, you know. Using a dictionary there is at the church. Then I started to see the threads between different observations. Finally, I was able to comprehend and appreciate the concepts, the methods, the techniques, the scientific assumptions. I must say, too, that my retired high school teacher helped me a lot. With his help, I was even able to write short essays that appeared in the 'Arqueología Mexicana' magazine."

"That is wonderful, Carlos. So, you and I share the same passion! It would be good if we could talk seriously about our common interests. You know. Work together?"

"Suits me fine!"

Rosa is delighted. Lady Luck is on her side! She has found a competent colleague specialized in local archaeology. Thanks to Consuelo's intuitive contribution. Could not ask for any better.

Carlos confirms "Those are one of the most elaborate cave paintings in the Americas. And they are right here, in our own backyard!"

Rosa echoes "I only have a small datation project. But, based on what you just told me, we could later write a paper about the Mulegé region and present it at San Diego University."

"Ah, yes? When?" interjects Carlos, all excited.

"The datation results are due at the end of the 2015 fall semester. But my long-term plan is to compare the graphic styles and petroglyph techniques used in the Baja cave paintings to those I worked on in France at Lascaux and in Algeria's Sahara Desert …"

"*Oops! One more slip …*" realizes Rosa secretly. "*No way, dear Rosa, can you let him know about your previous life, wherever you were. You do not want to lose such a good friend because of your silly lies! You need him!*"

Unaware of Rosa's embarrassment, Carlos jumps in, delighted "Oh, you went to France and to North Africa? Very interesting! There is a lot of work to be done there, too."

Rosa feels guilty but she sees no way out but to concoct another lie. "No, what I mean, Carlos, is that I studied pictures of those paintings when I was studying at the University, in Buenos Aires."

"Oh! I see …" Carlos says, wincing a bit, unable to hide a hint of disbelief. "If you are ever planning to go to Mulegé, I can show you around. There are two sites. One, known as La Trinidad, is relatively easy to access and now well-documented. The other, called Pintas Piedras, higher up in the hills, is more difficult to reach. That is the one you should explore and publish about … because it has never been documented in the professional literature. You would become famous!"

The two archaeologists - the pro and the amateur – do not feel the time go by, driven by their shared scientific passion.

Consuelo, either presiding from her rattan chair or pretending to be busy doing something or other, does not miss a word. Delighted to notice the 'chemistry' that is already brewing between the two, she purposely slides away, hoping that 'things' will get a bit hotter.

With Consuelo chaperoning now less evident, Carlos feels free to announce "I have to tell you something personal, Professor. I would have loved to have a family, with children. To restart the DNA chain of the extinct Guaycura people. But now, at forty-eight, it is too late for me. You see, I am the last direct descendants of the Guaycura people. I profoundly feel the instinctual need to regenerate my ancestors' life in these modern times. Using my own Guaycura DNA."

"Oh, Carlos, what you are saying is so moving. Without doubt those are deeply painful feelings."

"Yes. You are right, Professor. I apologize for letting myself go in such a personal issue."

"Please do not apologize. I simply understand. That's all." Rosa then adds, unable to repress a juvenile blushing: "And, by the way, I feel better when you call me Rosa."

"Well, to continue, Rosa," answers Carlos, while trying to hide his pleasure from noticing the sweet step in intimacy that has just been overcome so naturally. He goes on with passion "The Guaycura tribes were living in the Comondu region, north of here, just where Baja California Sur begins. I will take you there. You'll see. Beautiful. Cliffs with grandiose basaltic formations. And, in the verdant valleys below, trees and bamboos. My ancestors used those bamboos to make spears and arrows. Which explains why in 1532, the Spanish Conquistadors decimated them."

—◦/◦/◦—

One topic leads to another. Delighted for having found someone to talk about his feelings and professional passion for indigenous peoples, Carlos shares his dream with Rosa. "You know, Rosa, with the influx of tourists now coming into Baja, I am dreaming of setting up a Baja native museum in Todos Santos. Nothing big, of course. Because in Todos Santos, we already have the *Casa de la Cultura*. It would be something genuine. Only about native nations from Baja. Not split into groups but as a unified ethnic group joined into a common cultural entity. The tribes that managed to survive like the Pai-Pai, the Kumeyaay, the Cucapá, the Kiliwa and others in the north. Cochimi in the center. And in the south, the decimated Pericu, Monqui. And finally, the Guaycura who are extinct … except for me!"

"The Baja native museum will not be touristy. Nor will it be too 'professional' if I may say so, Professor. It will be for the general public. As a deserved tribute for Baja's ancient inhabitants who really knew how to share this slice of Paradise …"

"That would be great. I agree about the Paradise part, too," ventures Rosa "Hey, we could build that museum on this street, next to the hotel."

"You must be kidding, right?"

"No, I mean it" confirms Rosa. "It can be done. Perhaps you and I can plan that, sometime soon."

"That would be great, Rosa … You know what? It's already six." Carlos bends his head to check that Consuelo is not within earshot "See you tomorrow after church."

"Not too late, please!" whispers Rosa.

Casually, pretending to just come back, Consuelo appears at the door "After church. Yes, that will do, children!"

Numbed, the two friends exchange a glance, half embarrassed and half naughty.

LA LINDA CABANA LIBRARY – April 2014

Recently, Carlos has noticed some tension between Consuelo and Rosa. To promote peace, he has decided to take a pre-emptive action.

A cute reed cabana will do the trick. To put some space between the two … you know …

It will be built in the tiny, wooded section on the north side of the jalapeño field. There, way down, by the beach. With a view on Punta Lobos to the south.

A rattan table and two folding chairs create a peaceful corner. Both private and lost in nature.

"Come see what I built, Rosa. Bring your books. I'll bring mine. Let's do our own research work here, away from the construction site."

"Great idea, Carlos. You are so sweet. And so right. We both need a break! This will be our research library … The La Linda Cabana Library!"

As it turns out, the two enthusiasts find other topics than ethnology to talk about.

Both of the same age and with similar aspirations, they are excited to find tender commonalities in their respective lives.

The shared mid-mornings or early evenings ocean breeze is a welcome balm for both.

Amid books and manuscripts, a genuine friendship rapidly develops that they both openly welcome and cultivate.

To top it all, Carlos had the idea to introduce Rosa to Damiana, the refreshing local drink that runs down your throat so smoothly.

"Do you like it? Good, hey? I knew you would. You know, this liqueur contains a plant well-known by my ancestors. It's like tequila but much tastier. It uses the aromatic Damania **plant. The Guaycuras, like all Baja** *Indios***, were intimately familiar with their vegetal environment. As hunter-gatherers they knew their plants to a perfection. They exploited herbs, bushes, trees in their natural habitat, rather than cultivating them."**

"I like what you say about your prehistoric ancestors, Carlos. For a long time I have been trying to formulate for my own ancestors what you just said about the Guaycuras. Consuelo and you have opened my eyes to the need to revere our ancestors. Ethnologists in different disciplines study and analyse human remains as artifacts. I am beginning to think that the time has come to consider these beings as our relatives. We should admire them, respect them, love them. Humanity today would benefit from such an attitude. Clans, tribes, nations, recognizing their common ancestors could then abandon the idiotic habit of armed conflicts and wars and especially the pathetic terrorism now in fashion... So, Carlos, what were you saying about your beautiful flowers?"

"What you have just expressed are really profound ideas, Rosa. They formulate a seminal concept for a new branch in ethnology. By formulating more respect for its ancestors, humanity could reach higher levels of true development. About the Damania flowers, I'll show some to you when we go for a walk in the mountains. They are so beautiful in late spring. You'll see."

THE CASE OF THE JALAPENO FIELD – Apr 15, 2014

On one of those 'cabana library' evenings, perhaps embolden by one or two glasses of Damania, **Rosa decides to discuss the still unresolved jalapeño case.**

The sun has dipped gloriously into the Pacific. You might have seen what I am talking about. Just when, at the same time, a full moon peeps up in the East, on top of the Sierra de La Laguna Mountains, just a few miles away.

"Hey, Carlos."

"Yes, dear?"

"Since you know Consuelo so well, and since she likes you a lot, would you talk to her about the jalapeño field? This has gone on long enough. I really do not understand why this field means so much to her. Each time I bring the subject, she first goes into a fit and then gives me the silent treatment."

"Well, Rosa, this is one example of the deep divide that exists between your so-called western civilization and ours."

"Is that the case?"

"Yes, Rosa. As a paleo-ethnologist, you endeavour to look at humanity's past, right? Subconsciously you are looking for links, similarities between ancient dead people and yourself. Did you ever ponder why you chose this profession, this avocation, as opposed to any other one? "

"Good question, dear. I guess I could have been an accountant. Or a homemaker."

Rosa chokes and comes to an abrupt stop. Her heart pang hits her hard, as she mentally rehashes *"Oh, a homemaker. How do I wish …"* Talking to a good-looking man who seems to be interested in her, makes the 'old-maid' pain worse. She manages to continue the conversation. With a curt tone of voice that she immediately regrets, she says "Does not matter, really. The question at hand is the jalapeño field."

Carlos, aware of his faux pas, tries another approach "Rosa, in simple terms, I am just trying to identify the parallel between the Western and our indigenous world views."

Rosa struggles to find an escape. "That is a good point," she says out of despair.

Carlos, feeling equally awkward, can only go on with his scientific speech "I am glad you agree. There are great similarities between the two, despite superficial differences that are just like the thin lacquer that covers our identical psychological DNAs."

"You have very original concepts. Please tell me more, Carlos."

"Let me come to the point you have raised. Consuelo's is motivated by deeply rooted principles and beliefs about the dead. You see, Rosa, Consuelo cares much more for the welfare of dead people – in this case Señor and Señora Gomez – rather than for income, architectural appeal and convenience to the eventual guests."

"Thank you for telling me about these aspects of her … personality," mumbles Rosa, yawning.

Carlos, startled by the unusual platitude of her comment, comes to realize that Rosa is falling asleep. But he is surprised to hear her continue with a slurred voice "I am aware of that. And I do see the qualities of Consuelo's beliefs. In a brief time, she has taught me a lot about aspects of her mysticism. And I appreciate both her patience with me and your efforts to enlighten me, as you are doing right now. I think that I have improved a lot these past weeks."

"You did improve, Rosa. But do not go so fast. There is a deep chasm between observing ethnological differences, as a Margaret Mead would experience while studying the Papuan societies … and actually appreciating them, loving them, adopting them."

He realizes that he is coming on too strongly, moved by his own ancestral pains that he had decided to put on the back burner.

He continues with more reserve and a pinch of tenderness "It is good that you have an open mind. Do not worry. You have been with us just a short time. You have all the qualities you need to integrate yourself into our society, as it seems to be your wish: open-mindedness, sincerity and respect of others. "

He waits a while for a response. Noticing that Rosa does not have anything to say, he goes on "At all times, Consuelo thinks, decides and acts with one purpose in mind: that is to make sure that, even though they are physically dead, Señor and Señora Gomez have enough to eat and take care of their daily needs as they go through the tough travels through *Mictlan*, the land of the afterlife. Please understand, Rosa that, following death, a person has to go through harsh terrain and difficult obstacles. Each step they accomplish is a purifying trial before being allowed to reach the top level. That is where Heaven is. We, the living, must commune with them at all times to help them during those after-life efforts. That is why we must give them the kind of offerings we put on *ofrendas*."

"That is a beautiful explanation, Carlos. More beautiful than anything I have ever heard about other after-life concepts. It creates a genuine bond between the living and the dead. The end result is a profoundly human concept."

"I am happy you feel that way, Rosa. You and I were raised in the Catholic faith. It is a good thing. Because we are in a position to do our private brand of comparative religion ... For example, what we call *Mictlan* is exactly similar to what the Catholic Church calls the Purgatory. Do you see what I mean? ... Of course, you agree ... Both afterlife concepts are identical. But ours was followed for ten thousand years, right here in Baja. The Catholic version was conceived only fifteen hundred years ago. So, what rights do Catholics have to sneer at our own *Mictlan* beliefs. Just tell me!"

—✧✧✧—

This time, Carlos stops. He realizes that his pro-native harangue might be too harsh for the occasion.

Rosa does not answer, but simply nods her head softly, her eyes half-closed.

Encouraged by Rosa's half-approval, Carlos returns to his mystical comparisons "Let me come back to your point, dear. Consuelo has decided to keep the jalapeño field intact, not only out of respect for the Gomez couple she loved. But for their actual daily needs, as dead people who are laboring their way through Mictlan.

"On top of it all, you have to remember that Consuelo's soul actually hurts. The Gomez's were childless. Now in their afterlife struggles, they have nobody from earth to support them, except Consuelo. For Consuelo, it has become a priestly affair. Do you understand? "

Rosa remains silent, but her reposed expression seems to invite Carlos to continue.

"Do not worry, Rosa. I will now be your counselor. I will tell Consuelo that you, too, want to respect the Gomez's and sustain their afterlife travails. So, I suggest that you tell something very simple to Consuelo. Tell her that the new garden will include a beautiful patch of jalapeños. All kinds of jalapeños. All colors. Like a botanical garden, you know. To respect and feed the souls of the Gomez's. Tell her that you want Don Pedro's permission. And, you know what? If you say that, Consuelo will love you, and will let you have your garden of your dreams. As long as she can verify that all matters related to jalapeños are managed as promised to the souls of Señor et Señora Gomez. Do you understand?"

This time Rosa remains silent, eyes closed, motionless.

Carlos gets scared *"Did I serve her one too many* Damanias?"

After a while, her eyes still closed, Rosa whispers in a tender yet raucous voice "Carlos, do not say anything now. I see something. I will tell you later."

From across the table, Carlos extends his arms to tenderly hold Rosa's folded hands.

ROSA'S VISION ON APRIL'S FULL MOON - Apr 15, 2014

A good twenty minutes go by. The sun has left long streaks of deep red on the far-away horizon. The full moon, now spreading her generous splendor, has taken charge of the eastern skies.

Before opening her eyes, a faint smile on her lips, Rosa whispers "Yes, Carlos, now I understand."

Startled by her melodious and calm tone, Carlos realizes that Rosa wants him to sit by her side.

"I was naked. In front of a waterfall sparkling along a cliff. From a shiny round spring, on high. I walked into the falling water. The drops splattered gently on my skin. That is when I realized that I was not wet. It was not water. It was some kind of a glittering substance. I raised my whole face into the shower. That is when I felt physically elevated. Moved up towards the top of the cliff, into the round spring. Sucked up into the waterfall. Then I disappeared. Then I became the waterfall itself."

Carlos gets up, gently holding Rosa by her shoulders as she stands up for a deep embrace.

"I love you, Rosa."

"I love you too, Carlos."

"Rosa."

"Yes, Carlos?"

"I know where the waterfall is. I'll take you there. You and I come from the same fire. You just went through a transfiguration that is reserved to the very few."

"Yes, it was beautiful."

THE JALAPENO FIELD: CASE CLOSED – Apr 20, 2014

Somewhere along the line, Carlos decided to go double-duty on the repair project. Two neighbors have agreed to help, as long as Carlos gives them some of the concrete he just bought.

After the cleansing waterfall experience, Rosa feels like a lady of leisure, mentally invigorated by a new inner peace. She has decided to return to the research work that she has neglected for too long.

Before breakfast, she goes by the construction site with cups of coffee for Carlos and his helpers.

"Carlos, after breakfast, I am going to the La Linda Cabana Library. Will you join me later when you want to take a break?"

"Of course, dear. But only after washing my grubby hands. This cement has a nasty way to chew your skin!"

Back at the dining room's breakfast table, while munching a few bites of her *machaca*, Rosa raises her hand to get Consuelo's attention. "Consuelo, Carlos has explained something to me."

The brain of Consuelo-the-matchmaker goes into high gear. "Yes, I know what you are going to tell me, Rosa. I saw you two. You think I am blind or what? You are getting along in that library he built for your, right? So, tell me. Do you love him or what? I know he loves you. He almost told me that he does. Best thing is to say a prayer to Santa Maria de Guadalupe …"

After the short prayer, it takes a few minutes for Rosa to muster the courage to say "You are right, Consuelo, Carlos and I are good friends. But I want to share something else."

Consuelo spins around to face Rosa. She looks anxious, almost on the defensive. "Yes?"

"Carlos told me that, out of respect for Señor and Señora Gomez, the new garden should have a whole section with jalapeños only. All kinds of jalapeños. A beautiful garden of jalapeños that the visitors will enjoy."

"Not a bad idea." Consuelo is delighted but refrains from showing her satisfaction. She has to keep the upper hand, you see ...

Rosa feels the need to make an intimate confession. Hoping to find a way to put an end to her relentless pains.

She hesitates a while before sharing her vision and the interpretation Carlos has given her.

Consuelo is delighted. "Gracia Dios, hija mia, this is the real proof that the good spirits want to heal you. Then you will become the person you want to become."

"Thank you, dear Consuelo. I have something else to tell you. After the vision I had the other evening, and now under your guidance, do you think I should go to Don Pedro for therapy sessions? You know, to become a better person. To learn how to give respect."

This time, all Consuelo's defenses are down. "That is great, my child. That is just great. You are starting to be blessed. Learn how to respect the departed. And how to deserve their respect, as well. Then, they will protect you and help you achieve your own goals."

"Thanks to you, Consuelo."

"Do not thank me. Thank the departed. You see, Rosa. It was easy to decide about the jalapeño field, no?"

"Yes it was, Consuelo."

"Understand. The jalapeño field problem was irking you. You were upset and you got nothing, right?"

"Yes, that is correct, Consuelo."

"Well, Rosa, understand me. You think that you are the one who found that peaceful solution, right?"

"Yes ..."

"Wrong. Let me tell you. The good solution about the jalapeños is not from you. It is an idea you got from the departed, bless their souls. They appreciated your change of attitude. So, they told you what to think. They gave you a solution to your problem. The departed are starting to love you, Rosa. They want you to be true to yourself."

"Yes, that is a good lesson for me."

Consuelo comes back to the offensive "Now for your big problems, I will ask Don Pedro. He will know how to help you."

"Thank you, Consuelo," answers Rosa while thinking *"What does she mean about my big problems?"*

"Yes, yes … Thank me. That's good. Thank the departed, as I told you. But be careful, child. You cannot lie to Don Pedro. Do not lie, hear me? If you hide something, it is bad. If you lie, it is terrible."

"I understand," says Rosa automatically, while thinking *"Consuelo is right, Rosa dear. You do have a big problem. You are creating charades instead of facing your realities. It is not fair to Consuelo, and Carlos for that matter. They trust you. While you lie to them, for selfish reasons."*

Lying has become a way of life since she arrived in Baja. She had planned that immature approach while in San Diego. She thought that fibs would shield her from past pains. To hide her identity while trying to invent herself a new one. To be accepted in her new environment. Now, those cute fibs have created gooey webs that strain her relationship with Consuelo and Carlos. The Carlos she loves. The Consuelo she needs.

These thoughts trigger her usual panic attack. *"Rosa, Rosa dear. What will happen if Consuelo starts rejecting you just because you lie? You will not have anybody to depend on, in your pathetic isolated fake universe. And, O God, Carlos who always submit himself to Consuelo's decisions, will be forced to dump you. And then, you idiot? Then what?"*

To overcome her fear, she gives a tap to her deranged head.

"You are in denial. Denial is your downfall, Rosa. You must find a new way to confront your traumas."

Regaining her senses and her composure she concludes *"At least, to start with, stop denying your denial, for Pete's sake!"*

HURRICANE ODILE – Sept 10 to 17, 2014

The September 14, 2014 category 4 Hurricane Odile, with its 140 miles per hour, landed at Cabos San Lucas, just south of Todos Santos. It ripped most of La Linda's roof off. All doors, all windows were blown away, nowhere to be found. The city inspectors declared it unfit for habitation. Clients had to be refunded. Worst of all, management had to move out.

———⊲⁄⁄⁄⊳———

Consuelo collapses, shattered, just like her beloved La Linda.

The devastation is widespread throughout Todos Santos. Yet, many neighborhood houses were left intact.

"Why, why is it that only our La Linda was hit so bad?" repeats Consuelo, despaired, in search for a culprit. "This is a bad omen, Rosa child. First the *maremotto* and now the hurricane. This is your last warning. This time, the spirits at sea are terribly mad at you, you see, because you are the owner. I am only the manager. *Gracia Dios* the *ofrenda* corner was not destroyed. It is a miracle. This means that the spirits are giving you a last chance. Personally, I do not have anything against you. The spirits are angry. Not me. Come help me. You and I will move the *ofrenda* to my house. Only you and me. No one else is allowed to do this."

Rosa feels bad for the devastation and sad to see Consuelo so terribly depressed. But she cannot understand why she should feel guilty for a natural weather event. "You are right, Consuelo. We will do the right thing for Señor and Señora Gomez. I promise to do my share."

"That is good, my child. Let's do it," says Consuelo, broken. Come live in my house, Rosita. It is small. But we will setup a cozy corner for you."

"Thank you, Consuelo. I will feel so good, close to you. A real family."

———⊲⁄⁄⁄⊳———

Juanito will be in charge of the move, with Carlos' eager help. He helps his mother and Rosa in his old pickup truck after loading the precious *ofrenda* pieces and Rosa's personal affairs. They arrive at Consuelo's minuscule house, up the hill, near *Panteon Antiguo,* in the old cemetery neighborhood.

"I'll show you your new room, Rosa. There is space only for your bed and clothes. I have setup this little curtain around the bed. Be careful not to pull it too strong. You'll be comfortable here. I'm glad you can stay at my place while these horrible things are happening. But the first thing to do is for you and I to rebuild the ofrenda."

Rosa is deeply touched. In times of crisis, Consuelo proves to be a true friend "O Consuelo, I feel so good when I am with you. I love you, Consuelo, like a mother. Thank you for letting me live with you."

'eres bienvenida.'

"Where are my books, papers and cameras?"

"Carlos took them to his apartment for now. Because, here, water dribbles down from the ceiling when it rains too hard."

"Good."

Suddenly, Consuelo, usually so tough, breaks down into a deep sob "Oh, Rosa. Oh, Rosa. I am so sad."

Rosa, without a word, comes to hold Consuelo on her heart, just like her old friend had done the first day they met.

After the move, Consuelo decides to take a long vacation. She will stay at home. Severely depressed, she cannot bear the sight of her beloved La Linda crumbled down like a house of cards. Nor does she want to see it being replaced. And the poor Gomez's! Luckily, the jalapenos field was not ripped.

Gone is the real La Linda. Where she spent half of her life.

Gone is the dear La Linda that she loved and remodelled. To make her so pretty. She was so pretty, I tell you. The doors, the windows, the walls, and all. And the beautiful ofrenda, set up just right, and all.

BUILDING THE NEW LA LINDA – Sept 2014 to Jan 2015

Rosa feels excited and full of hope. Yes, sadly, her dear friend Consuelo mourns the old La Linda. But now, finally, she, Rosa, will be able to build the new La Linda of her dreams.

Work on the Nueva La Linda will start immediately. Secretly, Rosa hopes that the workload and the pressures will help her avoid her nightmares and her paralyzing fears. Boosted by those positive feelings, she takes charge of the rebuilding even though she never was involved in construction projects. She has a precise mental picture of what the hotel will look like, its architectural style, the number of rooms, the grounds. The bedrooms along the two floors will be set in an open semi-circle facing the ocean. At each end of that semi-circle will be two graciously blending extensions: on one end will be the management's living quarters; the other end will be for a garage and business services. She is visualizing the marketing approaches. La Linda will cater uniquely for newlyweds to ensure continuous occupancy. In a way, she behaves as if the new La Linda was already standing in front of the gorgeous white beach. She is confident that all difficulties will be surmounted, up to the last coat of paint.

Temporarily, the construction site office will be the Cabana Library. Surprisingly, it has been spared by Odile.

There is a major advantage for Rosa. The cabana is where she will be protected from the noises of the construction site: drilling shovels, riveters and others. She tries to bear the extreme pain caused by the unusual noises. She doesn't want to let her friends know. She reacts violently to every blow of the air hammers, to every rotation of the drills. It's weird. The pain disappears as quickly as it came. But after a series of blows, the pain build-up becomes unbearable. She has to leave, using any excuse. The Cabana-Library is the perfect place. People know it's her private place. And, fortunately, her dear Carlos built it in a slight ravine, away from the hotel building and partially protected from the noise of the construction site.

Architects and professional contractors from Los Cabos, are pleased to get generous under-the-table bonuses in sealed envelopes. They give Rosa the top priority ahead of other customers equally hit by the devastation. They make sure that the new La Linda will survive all future disasters, God willing. Hurricane-proof thanks to its steel beams, the hotel will be covered by a ten-year Lloyd insurance policy.

In the span of three short months, now deeply anchored in the rock, the new La Linda's frame has sprung up out the sand like a genie, to the neighbors' amazement.

———◁/◁/◁———

Rosa is delighted. She is finally able to work on the hotel, just as she wanted to do when she arrived on that fateful November 15, 2013.

No one else knows, but besides the good weather, Rosa's secret bank account has had a major influence on the overall success. Neither Consuelo nor Carlos show any interest for the financial aspects of the on-going reconstruction. But money helps a great deal.

Here, I have to tell you a secret. To cover her tracks and remain incognito, Rosa has a clever arrangement with the Todos Santos branch of *Banco Real de Mexico*. When in need of funds for this or that building phase or task, all she had to do is to make a privately coded phone call to the bank. A discreet courier would soon arrive at the construction site's Library with a plain manila envelope, for the needed disbursements.

Thanks to a limitless budget, good management, creativity and heavy doses of work, a miracle happened. By April 2015, the new La Linda is nearing completion.

Carlos has come up with a good marketing idea. To cover the early fall low occupancy period, he has proposed to target the international surfing fans. They flock to Todos Santos during the October 'Big Waves' season. This way, the New La Linda, the jewel of Magical Todos Santos, will never run out of customers!

Rosa feels empowered in ways she would never have thought, transforming herself from university professor to construction entrepreneur.

With so much accomplished, time has come to take a breather.

INAUGURATION OF THE LIBRARY-MUSEUM– April 2015

Always attentive to Rosa's needs, Carlos has secretly taken charge of the construction of a new 'brick and mortar' La Linda Research Library. It will replace the previous cabana. The bamboo cabana was romantic but not very convenient for serious work. With the help of Juanito, he has started to design and put together the museum of his dreams. Standing on neat pine tables, they have setup plexiglass exhibits to display artifacts, photos, books and descriptions about each of the Baja California native nations.

A poster announces the future creation of an educational program especially designed for young people.

In early April, Carlos decides to make an announcement. "Señora Vasquez, you are invited at a private inauguration of the La Linda Research Library Museum. Only for the both of us. Tomorrow we will extend the invitation to a few friends from the Post Office and the Todos Santos Chamber of Commerce."

"Wow! You have turned this into quite an event, Señor Romero."

"Yes, why not? You deserve it, Rosa. You proposed it when we first met, 'member? And guess what, I even have a bottle of *Damania*, a bucket of ice from the new kitchen freezer and two crystal glasses!"

"OK. So, what are you waiting for, *hombre*?" giggles Rosa, taking Carlos by the waist … and letting him do likewise.

Initially focused on business issues, the conversation rapidly turns into amorous and introspective dialogs.

"I do not know how to express my gratitude, Carlos. In a little more than one year after I arrived here, running away from San Diego, I feel soothing waves of self-fulfilment. That is thanks to you, in great part."

"I am aware of your changes, Rosa. And I fully appreciate your gratitude. But it has been a two-way street, you know. Your presence in my life has opened both my heart and my mind to horizons I did not know existed."

Rosa takes a while before responding "Aside from our love, the most important change for me is that the past is definitely behind me, now. Our beloved La Linda and the support you and Consuelo gave me have helped me discover creativity as an art form."

"What do you mean?"

"Well, things like interior decorating, business management. How to follow a cooking recipe. Things I had never done before. I have learned how to enjoy life … and how to sip Damania! Thanks to you and Consuelo, I have learned how to enrich my people contacts with the locals. I used to be shabby in that department … I now appreciate artisans, workers, neighbors and try to learn from them all the time. That's it. I now can express it. I am becoming one of the locals! What a great feeling …"

"Well, in return, I can report to you that those people you just mentioned all appreciate your generosity, your open mindedness, your architectural vision and your instinctive sense of management. The neighbors too, are happy to have you, the Argentinian lady, among them. They are delighted to see someone finally give a fresh look to their rundown corner of town."

"*Querido*, thank you for your generous comments. But let us be humble, too. A lot is left to be done. As far as my personal recovery is concerned, I still have a few onion layers to peel off."

"Of course. Of course, dear. That is the challenge of life, right? But, thank God, despite the obstacles, things are now going in the right direction. And this, Señora Vasquez, will be the last philosophical comment of the evening. I propose another toast."

"*otro trago. ¡A su salud!*"

"Good night now. Rosa. There is a lot to do tomorrow morning to prepare for the evening's official inauguration of the Museum. We'll have about twenty people. Starting at five thirty."

"Ok! Bring them in!"

THE CHAMBER OF COMMERCE MEETING – May 13, 2015

At lunchtime, the twelve members of the Todos Santos Chamber of Commerce is holding their Spring meeting at the Hotel California.

Up to recently, people in town have not given too much attention to the La Linda hotel because of its remote location and its 'bad luck' reputation. All that changed when Carlos inaugurated the Research Library, and when Rosa started to give informal open house tours of the nearly-completed La Nueva Linda. The whole community was impressed. Other Todos Santos hotel owners were intrigued and concerned to see their old shabby competitor suddenly coming back to life.

You have to know that for a few years, the Eagles' rock group lawsuits against the owners of Hotel California had further boosted Todos Santos' reputation as a tourist hot spot. Eventually, the lawsuits about the use of the 'Hotel California' song were settled to both parties' satisfaction. The international fame, added to the song's throbbing rock music and genial lyrics, took the song's ratings through the roof. The song 'Hotel California' was heard to the farthest corners of the world. Loads of hippies arrived from all corners of the globe, and especially from the US.

When news came out that the old La Linda building, partly destroyed by Odile, was going to be razed down, owners of other establishments in town were eager to see what the new "La Linda" would look like.

They had heard that the hotel was going to be a classy building with a definite European allure. Some even said that it was built in the Argentinian style. Shining in elegance and sobriety, La Nueva Linda is nothing like the area's hotels, characterized by their tropically colorful entrances. Even before its inauguration 'La Nueva Linda' is starting to reign supreme in 'Magical Todos

Santos'. Yet, being specialized in the 'honeymooners' niche, it is not in direct competition with other hotels. It is a win-win situation for all.

⟨⟨⟩⟩

Before the meeting, as is always the case on such occasions, the Chamber of Commerce members indulge in their usual non-stop gossips while the *cerveza* [beer] freely flows.

"Did you see what's happening at the beach?"

"No, what?"

"The La Linda!"

"La Linda what? Tell me."

"They razed it down!"

"That's bad luck, man. The poor departed Gomez! What will happen to them?"

"And who bought it?"

"Yes, who? Not a Gringo, I hope?"

"Believe it or not. A woman bought it."

"A woman? You must be kidding …"

"Yes, I tell you. She bought it. Cash!"

"Cash? She must be loaded …"

"Yes, I swear. The city owned it, you know. None of us wanted it because of the curse, right? And she tried to patch it. And then Odile tore it down. And now the new La Linda is almost finished."

"Where is that woman from? Surely not from here, Hahaha!"

"From Argentina."

"We do not see no Argentinians around here. Lots of Gringos, but nobody from Argentina! Hahaha!"

—<(✌/✌/✌)—

"Hey, Alberto, you know Carlos Romero the *Indio* letter carrier, right? He works weekends on the construction site there. Go tell him now. Ask him to invite the Argentinian beauty. We'll found out who she is. A buddy of mine saw her once. He tells me she is a looker. And single, on top of it all!"

"Hey, now you talk straight, man!"

"Hey, guys, do you agree? This Saturday? Here? All who agree, raise your hand.

Do I have double vision or what? I count twenty-four hands. For only twelve of us. OK. Enough bullshit, I will reserve a table for fourteen. For dinner."

WELCOME TO HOTEL CALIFORNIA – May 20, 2015

Coming back to La Nueva Linda from the market with a few things for the kitchen, Carlos cannot hold his excitement.

"Rosa, Rosa!"

"Yes, *querido*. What's the matter? I never saw you so excited! Tell me!"

"I just got a call from my buddy Alberto. As the owner of the New La Linda, the Chamber of Commerce is inviting you to a friendly dinner party."

"That's great! It will be a pleasure. You come with me, right?"

"Yes, of course."

"That's good PR work, Carlos. So, give me the details. Let me fill the appointment calendar. So, what day, what time?"

"Tomorrow, at 6:30pm."

"And where?"

"At Hotel California."

"What? No! No! … Absolutely not!" shouts Rosa. Her voice is so coarse and guttural, that it scares Carlos.

Instantaneously transformed from her normal jolly self, Rosa falls in sort of an excited coma. Sickly pale and shaking, she collapses in her chair and lays her head on her folded arms.

"Rosa, Rosa. What's the matter with you? Tell me. What can I do for you?"

Rosa straightens herself up in her chair "I am OK, Carlos. Do not worry."

"You are funny, honey. How can I not worry when things like this happen to you? Without any warning."

"I know that it is strange to you. I have a problem. I am in control of it. Believe me."

"Why do the words Hotel California put you in such a terrible state?"

"Please do not ever ask me that again. I am in symptoms, that's all. "

"You baffle me. You are in what?"

"In symptoms, Carlos. I will make the effort. For you. Tell Alberto that we accept the invitation."

"Thanks for the effort, Rosa. But I must warn you. I want a full explanation of what has just happened to you. Looks to me, there is something serious behind it."

"Yeah …"

"Rosa, I want you to promise me to give me a full explanation after the meeting. OK?"

"OK."

⟨◦/◦/◦⟩

The next day, at 6:30 pm, Carlos and Rosa arrive at Hotel California.

This is the first time that Rosa sees the famous hotel. She is surprised to realize that for more than a year in Todos Santos, she has almost never been in town, always staying at La Linda's. Especially, she had made a point to avoid Hotel California, fearing that the building itself could trigger a new episode.

To hide her sudden anxiety, Rosa pretends to be admiring the large ochre building. "So, that is the famous Hotel California? Quite a place. Too boxy. But impressive."

"Good architectural evaluation. Let's get in. I see the guys waiting for us," answers Carlos.

They zigzag through the crowds packed in the lobby and the sales room full of high-ticket trinkets. "Look, Carlos, this ceramic watermelon is so realistic!" "Yes, a friend of mine create those things. They are expensive. But cheap to make. I will ask him to give me one for free. For our lobby. Or something else of your liking, honey."

They enter the noisy hotel restaurant where their company is already drinking and munching hors-d'oeuvres.

Over plentiful servings of local dishes, introductions, polite talks and chats go on for an hour. Rosa tries her best to be sociable, answering questions about the La Linda, ending on a happy statement "We are going through the finishing touches and hope to have the grand opening in two weeks. You are all invited."

While the audience claps and congratulates, Rosa leans towards Carlos "Honey, I really do not feel good. Please ask them to excuse us."

—⋖०/०/०⋗—

On the way to the parking lot, Rosa feels a fainting spell go through her whole being "Carlos, hold me as we walk to the car."

"Of course, dear. We'll be home in no time."

"No, I will wait for you in the car. Please go to the sales room and buy a CD of 'Hotel California'. The song, you know."

"Yes."

Carlos knows that the hotel is not allowed to sell those CDs anymore. No problem. He can buy it from a street kid selling illegal copies on the sidewalk.

Rosa grabs the CD. She clutches it to her chest with a weird nervous gesture. Her voice is faint and flat "Now. When we get home, bring the boom box from the kitchen."

"OK."

"Then help me to my room. Do not say anything and leave me alone."

THE PTSD FLASHBACK–
Evening May 20, 2015

Rosa collapses on her bed, while Carlos unwraps the CD, inserts it, plugs the boom box.

Before leaving, concerned, he gives Rosa a light kiss on the forehead.

His first kiss.

He recoils in horror when Rosa rejects him with a raucous demand "Go away! Go away!"

Back in the downstairs living room, at a loss, he walks to the *ofrenda* for a prayer to the Virgen Maria de Guadalupe.

Hoping to soon get a call from Rosa, he prepares a pitcher of hot chocolate and awaits anxiously for a call or some sound from upstairs.

As soon as Carlos left her, Rosa is overcome by a horrendous anger. Turns the boombox on. To play the music she so much loves. First softly. Then louder and louder.

> *"What a lovely place … What a lovely face."*

She feels the soothing music comes back in her head.

Burning.

Louder!

> *'Up ahead in the distance'.*

She increases the volume. Louder!

> *'Up ahead in the distance. Tiffany-twisted'.*

She goes through the convulsion that she knows too well.

Then comes the cataleptic collapse.

> *'This could be heaven. Or this could be hell'.*

The pain let go.

The nightmare returns.

First it's a shiver.

It is not death.

Just nothingness.

Broken, wounded.

She does not exist anymore.

With a shriek, she sits up.

"Jim! Jim! The blood! The blood! Oh, the blood!"

While screaming she grabs the boombox with both hands.

Raises it over her head.

She feels the boombox being ripped out of her hands as if by some external force.

Smack into the mirror at the foot of the bed.

She can only see glimpses of her reflection in the curved shards as they fall to the floor and on the bed cover.

An eerie peace overcomes her.

—⫷ɔ/ɔ/ɔ⫸—

Carlos is now with her, looking at cuts on her hands and arms.

"I was downstairs praying for you, love. Do not worry. That's it. It's over. The bad spirits are gone, now. Rest. I will come back right away."

He is back in no time, balancing a pitcher of hot chocolate, a bottle of hydrogen peroxide, a big cardboard box and a broom.

"You see, I am all prepared," he says in a forced laughter.

"Thank you honey. I will help you to pick up the pieces."

"OK. Just take care of what's on the bed. Then we'll stop your bleeding. Nothing serious. The cuts are superficial. But I will have to tell Don Pedro. So that he can tell us the right thing to do."

"Oh! Carlos. I feel so ashamed for what has happened. I could not stop myself. You see, it was like Jim's mirror. I hated it."

Carlos is surprised. "Jim? Who is Jim?"

"I will never tell anybody who Jim was."

"I know, I know. The bad spirits. We will take care of that later. For now, it's all over."

"What I mean is that I feel bad because Consuelo told me that Don Pedro had blessed the mirror. And now I broke it. She will never recover from that!"

"Do not worry, honey. First, Consuelo is at her home tonight. Second, I have the exact same mirror in the garage. I had bought it when Juanito bought yours. Don Pedro blessed mine too. It has some stain. But it's OK. I will install it tonight. Nobody will know."

"Oh, that's good. With you I always feel better."

"But I will have to tell Consuelo. I should not lie to her, you know. She will understand when I explain. She loves you, Rosa. We all want you to be healed from whatever bothers you. We know you are an exceptionally good person. There are few people like you around, here. But we will have to send you to Don Pedro for treatment. This way, what you went through tonight will never happen again."

"Carlos. I will follow your advice. I am yours."

"Alright. Alright. Now let's take care of those scratches. You are lucky. No blood went on the bedcover. That would have been bad luck. That's it. Calm down. Have your chocolate milk."

"Thank you, love" whispers Rosa, now tucked in bed.

All of a sudden, as if talking to herself, Rosa says, "Yes, but here it is…"

She does not manage to finish her sentence.

"Here what? Tell me. Tell me."

"No! No! Never!"

Stunned, Carlos is baffled.

He sits on the edge of the bed, takes Rosa's scratched hand before continuing tenderly "Rosa, it's time to get down to reality. Our reality. You are suffering, darling. To put an end to your suffering, we must eliminate its causes, whatever they are. Only you can make the decision to talk. But you have to talk. Don't hide anything anymore. You have to tell me. You have to tell the world. You can't hide your terrible secrets anymore. If you continue on the path of silence, the secrets will break your soul. You can't accept that. I can't accept that."

Wearily, Rosa slowly nods her head.

Carlos gives his second kiss of the night.

On his lover's forehead.

DECIDING ON ROSA'S THERAPY – May 27, 2015

One week after Rosa's episode, Carlos had to go to Los Cabos, to buy concrete and roofing tiles from Ace Hardware. At home, Rosa feels exhausted. She is unable to control the stream of disturbing thoughts pop up randomly in her head.

Being apart for one or two days should not be a big deal for two middle-aged friends. But in the case of Carlos and Rosa, the separation raises sudden bursts of passionate enthusiasm. In ways that they had never experienced before. Like teenagers, any reason is good enough to start a phone call that goes on for delightfully long whiles.

—*◦/◦/◦*—

Rosa is in the La Linda Library. She feels tense, unable to control an uneasy anxiety. Her cell phone rings. It is Carlos.

"Rosa, I miss you, darling. It's too bad you did not come with me. We could have fun here. That would be good for you. There are lots of migrating whales passing around the cape today. I can see them right now from the hotel window. Sorry, but I have to stay in Los Cabos for two more days. A friend is giving us a whole bunch of beams. But they are not ready for pickup yet. Tell me, how are you? How do you feel?"

"Oh! I am fine. I am fine. But I miss you. Don't make it longer than two days, OK? There is something I want to share with you, love. The waterfall experience has made me feel a deep sense of inner peace. That is so new for me, you know. This new kind of calm is a bit scary. Can you explain that? I am not sure I can express how I feel, really. Cleansed? Freed? Sort of in a state of ecstasy. As if my body had gone out of this world and then came back. And then, after the dinner at Hotel California, I went through …. Well, you know better than I do. I feel that I have gone through a wall, or something like that. It is so weird."

—*◦/◦/◦*—

"You express your thoughts quite well, love. I am happy for you. According to our beliefs, that is to be expected. Yes, it is a new experience for you. That is because your soul is crossing into a new world. You must now internalize that awareness. Make it your own and at the same time, feel the intimacy of your contact with nature and its immensities. Through you."

"I follow you, Carlos. Tell me about the immensities."

"No, dear. This is not a right time."

"Oh, I beg you. Tell me about your immensities. I need to understand. I need to hear it from you. Now."

"Well, then ... I am talking about multiple-faceted immensities. They make a totality that regular mortals like you and I cannot even fathom. In fact, we, humans in this twenty-first century with all the knowledge we have amassed, are not further ahead than our stone age ancestors. Think about the immensity of the universe you and I watch at night on the beach. Down to the immensity of the sub-atomic particles in each grain of sand on the same beach. Through the immense complexities of your genome, your central nervous system and your organs. Try to develop the intimate physical awareness that every second, right now, from the depths of the universe, generated billions of years ago, billions of neutrinos come to cross, at the speed of light, each of the 30 billion cells that constitute your body."

"Wow, I never thought about that" says Rosa, mesmerized.

"That's it, Rosa. As a modern-day scientist inside your engineering paradigms, you have been trained to compartmentalize and dissect each of those aspects, as separate scientific observations dissecting them in ever-increasing details. In microbiology, in genetics, in astronomy and other sciences. But without even trying to consider their ramification for humanity, its past and its future evolutions."

"All of this is hard to absorb at one, Carlos. But I see that you are right." Rosa has uttered those few words distinctly but at an a surprising speed.

Even though startled, Carlos feels the need to complete his remarks "In the exact opposite way, we, the so-called 'primitive' people, we view the world from a different perspective. We integrate those universal facts and our human experiences into a unified whole that we attempt to integrate in our thoughts and daily activities."

Still at the same speed, Rosa's voice is now chopped. "Don't you think that it is time to see that both approaches are valid? The modern world attempts to discover and analyse. The ancient world attempts to feel and synthetize."

Carlos tries to calm Rosa without hurting her feelings "That is a good description, honey."

Without reacting to Carlos' concerned voice, Rosa rambles on "You know, Carlos, when I first came here about one and half year ago, I was lost... and spiritually naive. Since then, and especially at this very moment, I realize that our relationship has exceptional qualities. If you don't mind, I'd like to give you a glimpse. You and I come from completely different ethnic and cultural backgrounds. Yet our ways of thinking complement each other. Lately, I've been getting ideas about both of us and about life in general. Admittedly, no matter which way you look, the world today is not always a pretty sight. International chaos, racial tensions, oppression of all kinds, terrorism, wars, and rumors of war all reign supreme. These are the usually inescapable expressions of the brutal laws of nature. On the other hand, humanity, in a new phase of evolution, seems to be becoming more self-aware. Important scientific discoveries are continually made about the Earth and the Universe in an increasingly coherent whole. Thanks to the Internet, these discoveries are rapidly disseminated and put into practice by more and ... " Rosa does not seem to realize that, in her haste, she has not finished her last sentence.

Carlos gets concerned. He tries to arrive at a less tense conclusion "I follow you, Rosa. And I agree with you, although the subject requires deep reflection. Could we talk about that at later?"

Going on at the same speed, Rosa ignores Carlos' suggestion "These two trends are currently at a point of extreme confrontation. Without being presumptuous, I am beginning to believe that you and I are part of an evolution that is taking place among humans. Something similar to what happened during the Enlightenment, but on a larger scale. In the 18th century, Condorcet, a brilliant mathematician and philosopher, was already promoting equal rights for women and people of all races. Nowadays, these are the two most critical issues in human relations. Unfortunately, we must remember that the poor man ended his life in prison for his ideas. But maybe, just maybe... the time has come to put his principles into action. You and I could have a modest contribution to such a movement. There, that's what I think about sometimes."

Rosa's comments are clearly expressed, but she speaks so fast that Carlos has a tough time following her. He tries to find words to calm her down.

"That's right, Rosa. I get it. You really do have a big vision. Yes, you and I could be role models in our immediate circle. For now, your reactions prove that the full moon that night had a profound effect on your being. But be careful. You are in a delicate phase of your transformation. You will have to make a conscious effort to maintain and enrich the change that has taken place in you as a result of that magical evening. You will then discover your true self..."

══*/*/*══

After a long pause, Carlos measures his words before going on "Tell you the truth, all of this leads me to say something personal. The truth, Rosa, is that you need some psychotherapy treatment. Would it be OK with you if I tell Consuelo a little bit of what you just shared with me?"

Rosa feels suspicious. She whispers: "Why would you have to tell Consuelo about me?"

"Quite simple. Because she loves you and tells everything to Don Pedro, that's why," answers Carlos to reassure her. "With your waterfall experience and now your nightmare the other night, Don Pedro will surely be able to find the best therapy for you. Consuelo is the only one who can tenderly and lovingly explain your situation. You need a profound healing, *cariña*. That's all there is to it."

Carlos catches his breath before continuing "It may be, as well, that you need a good vacation. Perhaps a trip back to Argentina, if you feel homesick."

Rosa cleverly changes the subject after being reminded of her shameful lie about being Argentinian.

"Yes, Carlos. I agree to have therapy. I trust you. You led me tenderly, with a purpose. For my good. So, I give you permission. Go ahead. Talk to Consuelo and let Don Pedro know. But I have to confess something. I am curious and anxious too. What kind of therapy Don Pedro will give me. How is that done?"

"I am glad you asked. Your soul was shaped according to the Western beliefs and life concepts as practiced in Argentina, right?"

"That is true" interjects Rosa while thinking *"Shame on you, dear Rosa. Right when you have a chance to discover your real self, that stupid Argentina lie comes back to mess up your relation with Carlos ... Yuk! "*

"On top of that" continues Carlos, "you are trained as a university professor. Therefore, I imagine that you have a certain reluctance to be treated according to methods that are strange to you and contrary to your basic precepts. That is understandable. As a matter of fact, you must know that Consuelo and myself appreciate your sincere efforts to become one of us."

"That is sweet for you to say that. Thank you."

"All right. I will explain Don Pedro's therapy when I come back."

"Make it soon, *cariño*"

"I sure will, *mi amor.*"

—=(٥/٥/٥)=—

After the long phone call, Rosa returns to her bedroom. To relax. To reflect about her life's changes. From her window, she admires the sober semi-circular elegance of her Linda, symbol of her own rebirth. *"How much I need to have Carlos. Right now. Close to me ..."* Out of desperation, she decides to practice Dr. Caldwell's daily meditation and PTSD exercises.

The anxiety returns. *"Rosa dear, do you still believe in those exercises? Let's face it. They did not do you any good. For more than a year, now. That horrible PTSD phrase. I hate it. Ignored by a world that cannot face it. How many PTSD cases due to terrorism? One million worldwide? Across all societies. And doctors have no way to erase the pain of so many. Am I right? Am I wrong?"*

—=(٥/٥/٥)=—

'What a lovely place ... What a lovely face."

—=(٥/٥/٥)=—

WHAT IS A CURANDERO? – May 28, 2015

"Rosa, look what the UPS truck just dropped!"

"What in the world is it, Carlos? It's huge, for sure!"

"It's a surprise for you, dear," answers Carlos as he disassembles the crate. "I ordered it when I was at Ace Hardware the other day. Well, it is for the both of us to enjoy. It's a *chiminea*. An outdoor fireplace. This one is made of steel. The traditional ones are in terra cotta. And therefore breakable. This one will be sturdy."

"Oh, I see. In Argentina, we call them *braseros*."

"Is that so? Whatever the name, we will try it tonight. And later we can buy more for our customers to warm their night-time beach parties. What do you think?"

"Excellent idea."

In the evening, once the fire is well started, Carlos calls Rosa on his cell phone from the gate by the beach. "Time to come on down, honey. The sun just went down. Could you bring the thermos of hot chocolate from the kitchen?"

"Coming!"

Rosa arrives. "It's kind of cool tonight. Here is a blanket."

"Good thing to have in case we decide to cuddle, too …"

"You are right, my man!"

Already one hour after sunset, the quietness of the beach invites the two lovers for a long moment of silence that Rosa interrupts after a sip of hot chocolate.

"Carlos, Consuelo told me that I should start the work with Don Pedro as soon as possible."

"I support the idea, Rosa. It can only do you good. It could relax you. You know what I mean, right?"

"Yes. But I am anxious about the session's details."

"It will be a new experience for you. Your anxiety is normal. That's to be expected. So, do not worry.

"Some of Don Pedro's therapy will seem strange to you. I suggest that you ignore the weird part of it. And concentrate on the spiritual aspects, from his point of view, representing our whole community. That spirituality is what the western world has lost. It goes beyond religious practices."

"Thanks for the advice. Now, to come to my point, the other day, after I had my vision, you said that I had gone through a *limpia*. What is a *limpia*? Look, here is my deal: I'll serve you another cup of chocolate if you start telling me ..."

"Well, Rosa, I have to be honest. I believe in the benefits of *curanderismo*. I have seen many people get better after their treatment. The *curandero* or a *curandera* must be a good one, of course. Not a charlatan. Too many of those around. Especially since the tourism plight has fallen upon us. I will try to explain, even though, as I told you, I have been trained in strict Catholicism theology and practices. I do not know too many details about shamanism as performed here and throughout Mexico."

"Thanks for your honesty, dear. Tell me anyway, professor. 'Cause your student is totally ignorant ... and is eager to know. I am all ears."

"OK. Let's start with *limpia*, since you asked."

Carlos knows how important this moment is for Rosa. He scoots close to her to make her feel secure. And sits straight, out of respect for the seriousness of the topic.

"*Limpare* means cleaning. A *Limpia* is a ceremonial procedure. Kind of a baptism. You can think of *curanderismo* as our traditional healing art. Our *curanderos* and *curanderas* combine Catholic faith, religion, and prayers with a variety of herbs, massages, ointments and smoke from bundles of burning sage. Their purpose is to heal the patient. Their method is to re-establish his or her inner spiritual balance.

"The loss of our God-given spiritual equilibrium is seen as the cause of the patient's ailment. Whatever that ailment might be. Diabetes, drug addiction, stomachache, inability to conceive, fear, whatever. Everything is treated as a spiritual imbalance inside the patient."

"I see what you mean, Carlos. If you think of it, western shrinks do the same kinds of treatment for their patients with psychosomatic or mental conditions. Like cognitive therapy, guided meditations, Mindfulness, body awareness … When you think of it, modern psychiatry has pretty limited results as of now. Modern shrinks do not use talking psychiatry anymore. Instead, they experiment psychotropic compounds. Each year, miraculous drugs are found, manufactured, and sold by Big Pharma. Only to be discarded later and replaced with new, equally ineffective new miracle drugs. Meanwhile, the number of mental patients continues to increase."

"You got it, Rosa. To go further, I will try to give you a hint. From your western point of view. Within general traditional guidelines, each *curandero* uses his own methods. In his practice, Don Pedro blends the spiritual teachings of Jesus of love and tolerance, with prayers and incantations. He uses different smokes, feathers, eggs, and other objects, depending on the ailment. Those objects correspond, if you want, to what physical therapists call modalities. The healer first tries to analyse the patient's emotional condition – even if the ailment is physical. Then, in a holistic way, he attempts to relate to the invisible spirits who guide the lives of all living creatures. That's it, in a nutshell."

—=〈〉/〉/〉〉=—

"That is a good explanation, Carlos. Thank you. From what you said, here in Mexico, the *curanderos* have religious overtones to their practice. But, come to think of it, in the western world, many people believe that some invisible, yet supernatural powers are in charge of their lives. They do not admit it. But they do it. Just look at people in the US, for example. They guide their daily life decisions according to what they read in their newspaper horoscope column in the subway or at the office. Look the popularity of card readers, palm readers with or without crystal balls! It is not science, but many people do believe in such things!"

"Horoscope? Card? Palm readers? Crystal balls? I never heard of those primitive beliefs, Rosa. I was told that westerners strive on logic and pragmatic solutions. Sounds to me some of their concepts are kind of wacko, no?"

"Yeah ... You are funny, Carlos. I must admit that you are right. Hahaha!"

"Yes, like many other aspects of life, attitudes depend on what side of the divide you are. Divisions separate human groups, sometimes with terrible consequences. Well, to come back to your question, *curanderos* treat different kinds of diseases. Like *susto* or *bilis*. Patients with *susto* suffer from nervousness, depression, dull eyes because of a trauma like a nasty car accident, a mistreatment when they were kids or something like that. *Bilis* patients experience more mundane symptoms like stomach aches."

"Those are useful and profound explanations, Carlos ... as long as one think about them seriously."

"Oh, gosh! I have been rambling, again. Sorry. Now you see why people in town say that I am crazy. I talk too much when I get launched on topics that excite me. The result is that I have a tough time expressing what I want to say, when the topics become too complicated."

"No, Carlos, as I said when we first met, you absolutely are not crazy! And, sooner or later, every scientist comes to a standstill over the use of words that cannot correspond to his or her thoughts. This is when metaphysics come to the rescue."

"Crazy or not, here the answer to your initial question. The *curandero* attempts to cleanse the patient's soul and body of whatever hurts them. To chase the bad spirits that are the cause of all physical and nervous problems. The best treatment time is during a full moon."

"So, when I go for the session with Don Pedro, what I am supposed to say?"

"Not much. But only the truth, Rosa. The truth. About yourself and your personal pains."

Carlos waits for an answer.

None come from Rosa who seems dumbfounded.

"At the end of the session, Don Pedro will assign a *limpia*."

"Oh, I see."

"Rosa, I do not have my watch. The way the stars have turned in the sky, it must be very late!"

"I do not have mine watch, either."

"Let's go home. If the night beach cops come by, they will think we are bums and take us to the clinker. I'd rather sleep in my bed."

"Me too, darling."

DON PEDRO'S THERAPY SESSION –
June 4, 2015

Today, Carlos was first at the staff breakfast table.

"Hey, Rosa," says he, as his friend steps down from her second-floor apartment.

"Yes, dear?"

"Did you notice the full moon last night?"

"Yeah. It was so bright, shining through the window. I had to pull the venetians down."

"Is that all you have to say about June's full moon?"

"Yeah … am I missing something here?"

"Yes, you are, honey. Today is your appointment with Don Pedro. On June's full moon. It is an important sky event. To be respected."

"Oh, you are right! I completely forgot. Sorry. It's at six this afternoon, right? Gosh! Time has flown by since we talked about that. I have been feeling so good, too. But do not worry. I remember everything you taught me about his therapy methods … I remember, too, that you told me that, at some later time, I will go through a *limpia* treatment. Tell me. Any last-minute tip?"

"You do not have to prepare for anything. Don Pedro will lead the session, talking with and to the spirits. You will not have to say or do anything. Just sit there while he performs his mystical functions over you and through you. At the end of the session, he might or might not tell you his diagnosis. Diagnosis is not the right word. We should say that he might share with you how successful he was with the spirits communicating about your soul's condition. And again, he might not say anything at all. Depending."

"Thank you for giving me this refresher course, dear. I'll be ready at five."

"Good. I'll pick you up. Don Pedro lives in the Cabessa Blanca neighborhood. A mile or so up the hill, to the East. Not far from Consuelo's house near the *Panteon Antiguo*. Now, I have to go buy some meat and some fish for the kitchen. We have a full-house today. How do you like the new sous-chef I hired?"

"She is quite good. There is so much competition these days among hotels and restaurants. Finding a good chef is difficult. You did well, Carlos. I liked her grouper tacos yesterday. And so did the guests. The red salsa and the white sauce were complementing the fish to perfection. It was a pleasure to see so many people enjoy their dinner!"

Carlos and Rosa arrive at Don Pedro's at six sharp. In the middle of an open field, the windowless house is just a small cube covered with glossy white adobe. It has an eerie, almost supernatural appearance.

Consuelo is standing by the door, waiting for them.

"Just as when she was waiting for me in front of La Linda the day I arrived" giggles Rosa to cover her nervousness.

"Rosa," remarks Carlos while parking the car, almost scalding her "This is a sacred event. Nothing to kid about."

Instead of getting out of the car right away, with the door half-open, he continues in a stern voice: "You must understand that Consuelo is here because she cares for you. She wants the best to happen to you. Consuelo cares for all of us in Todos Santos and beyond. She has a gift from God to link people and good spirits and to extirpate the bad ones. That is why she is Don Pedro's assistant. "

Carlos goes on "You should know by now that, for Consuelo, managing La Linda is not a job. It is a priestly vocation. That is why she was waiting for you when you arrived. That is why she is here now. That is why you and I are together."

Rosa remains silent, contrite for her casual remark about Consuelo. On the spot she realizes that there is some kind of a lack in her personality.

At the same time, though, Carlos' thoughtful words have dissolved her nervous apprehension. Yet the weird going-thru-the-wall sensation returns.

Consuelo tenderly takes Rosa by her right hand to usher her into Don Pedro's treating room after crossing the small all-white courtyard.

Carlos stays in what looks like a waiting room, set with single-board benches secured on all four walls.

=◊/◊/◊=

Right away, as she steps in, Rosa physically feels Don Pedro's dark eyes scrutinizing her from head to toe.

In a strange symmetrical way, Rosa's scientific mind goes automatically into its analytic mode. She has received many an accolade from her colleagues over the years for that innate intellectual capacity. Not one detail of Don Pedro's appearance escapes her trained eyes.

In his bare feet, Don Pedro is sitting cross-legged on a colored carpet laid on a wide straw mat. In his ample *Machuy* white cotton pants and shirt, he exudes a sense of sanctity and assured repose. Wiry, he seems vigorous and agile. He has the same type of copper-tone skin as Carlos. Heavily wrinkled. Yet ageless. The only symbol of his profession is a cap or rather a wide hand-sewn head band fashioned from a furry wild animal.

After a few minutes of inspection, Don Pedro gestures, inviting Rosa to sit down. Consuelo, who has been sitting on one of the wall-mounted benches, brings a cushion for Rosa, as she squats gingerly. The cushion is similar to the ones Dr. Caldwell recommended for the meditations ... Rosa, who has stopped kneeling during her meditation practices for a while, feels her knee joints cracking. Luckily, they do not hurt. She ends up in the kneeling position, hands on knees, just two feet away from her silent therapist.

While Rosa was anxiously listening to her cracking knees, Consuelo was busy preparing bundles of sage smudge sticks. The kind that Carlos mentioned in his mini-course on *Curanderismo*. She sets two sticks on fire. A thick smoke invades the whole room. Rosa can barely distinguish Consuelo who has added other herbs and incense while walking around the room and chanting some harsh-sounding psalmody.

Don Pedro's deep voice comes through the smoke

"¿Cómo te llamas?"

"Rosa Vásquez."

"¿De donde vienes?"

"De la ciudad Orán, en Argentina."

A long period of silence follows.

As the smoke dissipates, Rosa scans the room without moving her head. Out of curiosity.

An incredible variety of implements are meticulously arranged on the floor, tables, and shelves. Having seen how well organized the *ofrendas* are at the hotel and at her home, Rosa is certain that Consuelo's hand is the one who transformed the apothecary chaos of herbs, candles, ribbons, feathers, stuffed animals, eggs, ornaments, gourds and whatever else, into an artistically attractive arrangement.

For some reason (was there some hypnotic compound in that smoke?) Rosa starts to feel dozy. Yet mentally alert. Don Pedro stands up slowly and, in a grave voice, intones long and incomprehensible incantations. Like an operating room nurse, Consuelo passes different implements that Don Pedro adroitly uses over Rosa's head, back, arms and legs: rattles of different colors and shapes, eggs, multicolored feathers. Or just empty hand fluid gestures. At Don Pedro's request or perhaps just on cue, Consuelo lights up candles and starts burning some plant fetched from a distant shelf.

Rosa, at the center of that ceremony, feels both uneasy and secure. Never in her life has she received such intense attention.

Suddenly silence and calm return to the room. Consuelo straightens her dress before returning to her bench.

Don Pedro squats back on his square carpet.

"¿Cómo te llamas?"

[What is your name?]

"Rosa Vásquez."

"¿De donde vienes?"

[where do you come from?]

This time Rosa decides to not lie about her origin.

She does not answer.

A feeling of peace invades her.

———⟨ɔ/ɔ/ɔ⟩———

Consuelo, noticing that Rosa's knees refuse to unfold after the prolong squatting, comes to help the patient stand up.

"Thank you, Consuelo. Will you come back home with us in Carlos' car?"

Consuelo is offended. She bends toward Rosa and whispers in her ear.

"Shame on you, child. Show some respect. You should not talk like this, now, about such a trivial thing, at a sacred moment ... But yes, I will. Step out and stay a while in the courtyard with Carlos. And do not talk. I must now ask Don Pedro what he has decided for your case."

Not a word is exchanged during the ride back to the hotel.

DON PEDRO'S DIAGNOSIS – June 4, 2015

The next day, at the staff breakfast table, Consuelo opens the conversation. "Hey, you two. Come with me. Yesterday was important for us all. No matter what the result. Before breakfast, let the three of us say a prayer. We want to thank Santa Maria de Guadalupe for our wellbeing and Rosa's presence among us all."

Holding hands, the three friends stand in front of the *ofrenda*.

'*Virgen Santísima de Guadalupe, Madre de Dios, Señora y Madre nuestra. Venos aquí postrados ante tu santa imagen …*

[Most Holy Virgin of Guadalupe, Mother of God, our Lady and our Mother. We come here prostrated before your holy image… "]

Not knowing the prayer, Rosa can only listen.

"Children," says Consuelo "I have to tell you what Don Pedro said. Some is very good. Some is just good."

⸺⟨⟩⸺

Across the table, Rosa and Carlos tensely wait for the verdict.

"Don Pedro knows that you are a good person, Rosa. He wants to cure you. Yesterday he was not able to wrench the bad spirits out of your body. He was happy that, the second time, you did not answer his question about where you are from. Your silence shows that the bad spirits are still inside you. But they were weakened by his treatment. And because of that short silence, Don Pedro wants to give you a second chance. Something will happen in the future. He has no idea when. Maybe months, maybe years. It will happen at the time of a full moon. The good spirits know your efforts. They will drill a tunnel through your skull to reach your soul. The bad spirits will be expelled through that tunnel. It will take one or more nights. That will be your night-time limpia. Then you will be free and clean forever. For now, Don Pedro said that you should continue your daily life in the company of people who love you. They too, care for you and help you through your journey. While you rest and think about your life, remember to think about and respect your departed. All of them. Many generations back. Even the ones you never knew."

"Thank you, Consuelo" say Rosa and Carlos in unison.

"And now let's have breakfast. There is a lot to do for the guests today," concludes Carlos. "Rosa, I would like to add a little note. I did some Google research yesterday. In terms of modern psychotherapy, Don Pedro and Consuelo are going to help you do a catharsis. It will be at night."

"A nocturnal catharsis? Yes, that's should the right term. I am ready!" jokes Rosa.

ENJOYING THE NEW LA LINDA – May to Sept 2015

This year, Baja's summer started in early June, right after Rosa's PTSD crash. In a supreme effort, she decided to forever erase that event out of her mind. She knows too well why the episode happened. Nobody else knows. Not even Carlos. Even though he lovingly helped her out of it and removed all physical traces.

On the other hand, Rosa tries to relive, as often as she can, the soothing feelings she experienced during the 'waterfall' experience. She savors remembering the sound of Carlos's voice when he said "I love you" for the first time.

Consuelo makes sure that Rosa sticks with Don Pedro's recommendation to take it easy. She does not say a word about therapy but showers Rosa with all kinds of motherly attentions.

Rosa is aware of the positive changes in her behavior thanks to all those positive influences. She has switched from compulsivity to what Dr. Caldwell calls 'enoughness' meaning 'what you are, the way you already are, is enough. No need for more compulsive search for unattainable excellence'.

She lets herself be lazy, alone in the garden or in her bedroom "I am now the full owner of a charming Baja hotel. Business has picked up beyond my expectations. The new La Linda is my own creation, the embodiment of the dream I had during my therapy in San Diego. I respect and am respected by the locals. I respect and am respected by my associates. I love Carlos and he loves me. Thanks to Don Pedro's therapy, I am now living the most precious part of my life.

"How sweetly naïve was I two years ago on that November day when I arrived here! I now know. I fabricated a bunch of fibs to cover my tracks. But let's face it. Telling those fibs was an escape for me. I enjoyed being that silly, carefree little girl I was never allowed to be. The little girl enjoyed the naughty fibs that fooled people. I used the fibs to protect myself. In fact, they were suffocating me."

After Don Pedro's therapy, bad memories from the horrid PTSD crash, when she broke the mirror, are now safely tucked away. Before that, in April, the positive turning point in her life was the waterfall experience that led Carlos to declare his love. *"He loves me! He loves me! Oh God! And I love him so much."*

She now feels alive.

Love and acceptance.

Those are the intangible factors of her recovery.

"It's time to enjoy life, Rosa dear. Go for it!"

Yes, la Señora Rosa Vasquez, owner of the new La Linda can be proud of many achievements during the summer months, as business runs smoothly with clockwork precision. Consuelo's idea to cater to honeymooners was the best advice ever. The funky real-estate agent was absolutely right: Consuelo is the key to La Linda's success. All obstacles, including a hurricane have been surmounted.

Rosa is now thrilled to offer ultra-modern conveniences to a never-ending flow of clients. Initially, she was not in favor of having excessive frills. She did not support the idea of the in-room Jacuzzis, the extra-wide king-size beds with heart-shaped spreads and cupid decorations. But Carlos and Juanito won the argument "You either have the furniture that clients like, or you will end up with empty rooms." Humbled, Rosa accepted. And now, she secretly envies the guests' intimate pleasures that she never enjoyed.

Separately, the one bone of contention between Rosa and Consuelo has been resolved. Consuelo has approved the friendly settlement with the jalapeño farmer. Imagine that! In payment of a salary equal to his field's income, he will be responsible to maintain the garden's botanical section, including the artistic jalapeño corner that is starting to become a local attraction in its own right! On top of it all, packets of blessed jalapeño seeds are sold at a counter of Carlos' Baja Natives Museum. As a result, everybody is happy: the farmer, her departed friends Señor and Señora Gomez, Consuelo, Carlos and of course Rosa.

Hotel responsibilities are smoothly divided.

Consuelo feels good for being the unchallenged 'manager', in charge of the customers' well-being – food and all needed amenities.

Piously working over many days, with Rosa's help, Consuelo has setup a new beautiful seven-tier *ofrenda*. The spiritual well-being of all in the hotel is thus assured, forever. Many clients and especially the young brides, at a significant moment of their life, yearning for immediate pregnancies, can also enjoy the good omens emanating from the *ofrenda's* statuettes and inspiring mementos.

Carlos, as the property manager, is efficiently in charge of general maintenance and vendors' coordination.

Juanito has been hired as manager of guests' entertainment … and bouncer in case of drugs- or booze- induced troubles. Thanks to his hands-off contact with his deceased brother Alessandro's drug gang, the hotel is under a tacit protection contract from the bad elements now penetrating Baja. His outgoing personality is just what the guests expect during their one-week stay. In particular, the open fireplaces set on the beach at night, are the favorite of all amorous couples.

We must not forget Carmensita, Consuelo's daughter. She is now an experienced chef, with an innate sense of culinary management that allows her to run her kitchen, her sous-chefs and her cute waitresses to the great pleasure of couples hungry after their long private romps.

As the CFO, Rosa supervises the whole show, in charge of marketing, sales and what not.

The business work, kept to a minimum, keeps her smoothly busy. Just enough to not interfere with her research project. She spends most of her mornings from breakfast to noon, in the La Linda Library. Hotel guests and visitors are allowed in the Library only in the afternoon. Carlos joins her every so often. The internet connection is not always good, but it does help them better prepare their expedition to the Mulegé caves, planned for some time in the fall.

The new wide-open U-shaped 20-suite hotel surrounds the delightful Baja-native Cactus garden, augmented with the mandatory jalapeños section on the north side. This open layout allows all second-floor rooms to offer the guests a full view of the ocean, from dainty balconies made-for-two.

Inside, each suite has its own romantic spiral staircase. Carlos designed the concept. For a reason that nobody was able to figure out, these spiral staircases are one of the most popular attractions for newlyweds.

The downstairs is reserved for the homey kitchen-dining room on one side. The other side offers elegant private or group lounging sections.

A sparkling pink oval swimming pool invites couples who do not feel like dipping their toes in the ocean waves. From the pool on down, the garden cascades to the shore, inviting adventurous guests for beach activities of their choosing.

For architectural continuity and operational convenience, a side building is seamlessly attached to each wing of the U-shaped hotel. The one on the right is for staff living quarters. The other is a garage-warehouse.

Designed by an expert horticulturist friend of Carlos, the garden spreads from the hotel down to the beach. Maintained by the farmer, it is adorned with lovely gazebos, water fountains and secluded benches. The gentle slope leads to the beach through an elegant, gated entrance towards the ocean, with view to the impressive Punta Lobos cape, as described in La Linda's advertising pamphlets.

It is in that heavenly garden that, most every day at sunset, enlaced in Carlos' arms, Rosa finally feels totally secure.

She delights to hear the faint giggles and amorous whispers coming from the loving couples passing in the dark on their way uphill. *"It's so good to see them having a good time. They are building lasting memories of their own. It is thanks to your work, Rosa dear. Thanks to your determination and the loving support of your friends. Be happy and proud of that. Coming to Miraculous Todos Santos was the best decision of your life!"*

For the first time in many years, she enjoys the inner peace she had tragically lost.

She has built her own nest. At the end of the world.

No need to hum the tune anymore.

Protected by Carlos, no one can ever harm her again.

PLANNING THE EXPEDITION –
Sept 7, 2015

The first week of each month is Carlos' turn to fix the staff breakfast.

Today, the only other 'staff' member is Rosa. Consuelo has been at Don Pedro's for the past two days. Juanito has gone with his wife Josefina to a friend's wedding in Los Cabos. And Carmensita does not come until 8, anyway.

At 6:30 am, Carlos has already fixed the coffee and *chilaquiles*, Rosa's favorite breakfast dish. For some reason, since last June, she has developed a liking for hot salsa. In particular, she cannot resist the sunny-side up eggs on top of tortillas fried in salsa. Especially if Carlos is the one who fixed them!

"Did you notice, Rosa, it's already down in the eighties!"

"Quite a change from last month's nineties. This way we can turn the central air-conditioning down. The summer electric bill was way too high for our budget" answers Rosa-the-accountant. "We cannot control the AC in the guests' suites. We might have to increase the rates, next season. But we can set the downstairs temp at seventy-two. What do you think?"

"Sounds good to me, dear," says Carlos. "But let us remember that the kitchen opens directly into the dining room. This creates a big thermal load. We did not think about that with the architects."

"Good point. Maybe we should install a double swinging door. By the way, who is cooking today since Consuelo is not here?"

"Carmensita," Carlos continues "Which brings me to what I have been wanting to tell you since last week …"

"OK, shoot!" interjects Rosa, teasing.

——《0/0/0》——

"One year ago, 'member?, Odile was ten miles at sea, churning its way before landfall at Los Cabos as a category 4. We, and especially you, honey, have accomplished a lot, since then. The next hurricane will not be able to zap the steel frames you have chosen for the new La Linda! Kidding aside, I want to share a personal plan with you. By personal, I mean for the both of us."

"Yes, Carlos. That sounds interesting. I am all ears."

"This is an El Niño year. There will not be any major weather perturbation coming our way. This will give us the opportunity to do two things. First, both of us can finally take a two-week pleasure vacation. And second, we can combine the fun time with the research work at the Mulegé murals."

"That's a great idea," answers Rosa. The timing is perfect. I have just received the paint sampling kits from San Diego University. And, most importantly, the authorization from the *Instituto Nacional de Antropología* in Mexico City. It arrived just yesterday. Believe it or not, I had filled the application forms back in January! They took nine months! Thank God they approved the trip and authorized us to take up to fifty specimens for analysis and carbon-14 testing. I was planning for next month. But now is just as good a time. I agree with you. Let's go!"

"Good. All suites are booked until December. Some people are postponing their weddings just to be sure they have a suite here. Consuelo, her daughter, Juanito and Josefina won't have any problem to run the place on their own. They will have to. There is no cell-phone coverage where we are going, you know. This way, we will be worry-free for a while! Alone at last …"

Rosa turns her head, pretending to fetch something or other "*Did you hear that, Rosa dear? He said: 'Alone at last'. Hide your silly flushing cheeks, you prudish girl …*"

The two vacationer-archaeologists go to work to prepare the trip.

On top of the list is the rental of an all-terrain vehicle. Then comes the purchase of camping equipment.

"Hertz can deliver the Wrangler here for a small charge. For the blanket and waterproof duffel bags, I know a fellow in Los Cabos. He has a military surplus shop. Brand new things. He showed me the bags last month. I can get them tomorrow. Oh! I almost forgot! We will need towels to dry ourselves if we decide to wade across the small creek we have to cross to reach the second site. I have found super-absorbent microfiber ones on Amazon."

"The creek?" Rosa is surprised. "We must cross a creek? I cannot swim, Carlos ..."

"Don't worry, honey. You'll see."

Rosa-the-scientist regains her composure.

"Yes, all is good, honey. I am scared but I trust you. But we will have to test those waterproof bags of yours before we go. What about dunking them in a tub for a long while and see if the inside stays dry? The tools and especially the specimens must stay completely dry. No humidity at all. If the bags fail the test, we will not go through that famous creek of yours. Right? I have to tell you, thinking about creeks gives me goose bumps. Is there another way?"

"No. No way to avoid the bath to go to the second site. At that spot the cliffs on each side come together. We'll see. Now, could you show me your equipment? I have to size the whole load. To buy the right size water-proof bags. Could we wrap the tools in our clothes or the towels?"

"Oh, no. Each piece of equipment must have its own small waterproof bag. But do not worry. Besides the camera, there are very few things. Let me go to my bedroom. I'll bring the tools. So you can check yourself."

⸻◈◈◈⸻

Rosa returns from her upstairs apartment.

"Here are the cameras and the tools. We have two of each of these, in case of loss, you know. Foldable hand lens, a bunch of brushes, chisels of different hardness, one medium and one very small pick, and a waterproof notebook. And, of course, the specimen box. That's all, really. Oh! Let us not forget the Institute's authorization. It will have to be in its own waterproof shipping tube. You know what? Let's use Ziplocs for the tools. They will be perfect, inside one of your super-duper military waterproof bags."

"I am very impressed by your professional pragmatism, Doctor Vasquez," says Carlos while pecking a kiss on his lover's cheek. Instead of turning her head away, as she has sometimes done, Rosa says "I liked that kiss, Mister Romero!"

"My pleasure … " Carlos reacts with a big smile, before returning to the next planning step.

"Wear thick camping clothes, including hiking boots and hat. I bought a thick 60 feet nylon rope at Ace Hardware. I will take care of the food and utensils. Enough for four days on the trails and on the road. So, do not worry about those things."

"My turn to be impressed! You have covered all points, sir. Great."

Carlos squints his eyes to mimic a flirting surprise "Hey, Rosa. There is something important that we missed. Or did we perhaps subconsciously skirt the issue?"

"What is it, *cariño*? Looks like you have covered all bases, no?"

"We have not made lodging arrangements, that's what we have not done. Usually Important for travelling couples, don't you think so?"

"Am I supposed to blush for that critical omission?"

"You are funny, Rosa. Blush or no blush we have to decide about where to stay. I have a suggestion.

"I have a good friend in La Paz. For the past twenty years we alternate. I visit him one year. He visits me the next. His name is Sebastian. He is Cochimi. He is lucky. Married. With eight kids! You will like his wife, Rosa. Sebastian owns a fish business. For our lodging in La Paz, I propose the Colonial Hotel, by the beach."

At this point, Carlos decides to start a more forceful approach "We'll relax and take it easy. We will do what tourists do. You know, lazy mornings together, brunch and museums in the afternoon. The short question is: one or two rooms?"

"Two." Rosa's abrupt answer is loaded with a heavy dose of insecurity.

This time, she cannot avoid being embarrassed. She feels a blush coming from her neck, up to her cheeks. *"Oh no, Rosa dear. I hope he does not notice!"*

"OK. Two rooms, if you say so." says Carlos, calm but obviously disappointed. "Then in Mulegé, we will stay at a B&B I know. Sorry, only one room, there.'

"All right, then." Rosa tries to paint a timid smile on her anxious face.

Carlos turns his cell phone on. To proudly show Facebook photos of the Colonial Hotel in La Paz and of the B&B in Mulegé.

In a desperate attempt, Rosa tries to recover from her previous gaffe "Those are lovely places. Good choice, Carlos. We will have a good time, for sure!"

Carlos tries to ignore Rosa's flat answer, so different from the one he was expecting to get after his multiple advances. "What do you think about leaving early Thursday morning? Without rushing on the way, we could be in La Paz by noon time. After one week in La Paz, we'll have four hours on the road to reach Mulegé."

Rosa, ever so precise, pulls her calendar. "Please confirm. We leave Thursday. One week in La Paz up to the 22nd and then to Mulegé, the datation work and return her on the 29th."

"Sounds good to me. I will make the hotel reservations and call my friend Sebastian. Then, tomorrow, I will tell Consuelo and Juanito. Right now, I will call Hertz for the Wrangler. It will be fun to drive that over the trails there! "

Consuelo and Juanito arrive just before noon, in time to serve the guests' lunch.

Rosa greets Consuelo. She does not remember having been so enthusiastic for a long, long time "Consuelo, Consuelo, guess what? Good news!"

"What good news? How can something happen when I was not here? Did you win the lottery?"

"No. I do not play the Loteria."

"Are you pregnant?"

"No, Consuelo. I am not pregnant. Stop teasing me. That's not fair!"

"So, what is it, my child?"

"Carlos and I are leaving Thursday morning."

"Where to?"

"La Paz for a week and then another week in Mulegé to visit the rock paintings."

"*¡Muy bien! ¡Muy bien!* " jumps in Consuelo. "You guys are really stuck with those painted rocks. Did you hear, Juanito?"

"Did I hear what?"

"They are going for a two-week trip. You know what I mean, right? I told you, did I not? I knew it. I knew it. And then, when they come back, something beautiful will happen to our lovebirds."

"What day will they be back, mother?"

"The 29th. "

Juanito goes to the kitchen wall calendar. "The 29th will be a Monday," while Consuelo continues, all excited "I will pray to Santa Maria de Guadalupe for the special blessings a man and a woman need in cases like this ... Muy bien! That's what I was hoping for. It took them too long. It was a lot faster than that in my days. Young people are so lazy, I tell you."

—◁/◁/◁—

Rosa, embarrassed by all the fuss she created, walks close to Consuelo and whispers "I have to ask you a little help."

"Go ahead, child."

"I want to buy a small gift for Carlos."

"Already?"

"Do not tease me, Consuelo. It is just a book."

"A book for a gift? You crazy or what?"

"Yes, look at it" says Rosa, opening her cell phone to Amazon's web page.

"*Dios mio*! I cannot read, Rosa. You know that."

"That's all right, Consuelo dear. Just look at the picture of the book."

"Yes, this looks good. What is it?"

"Well, it has pictures inside. By a famous professor. I am ordering it from Amazon. The package will arrive while we are gone. Addressed to Carlos himself. Just accept it when it arrives."

"That is nice. But what does the book say?"

"'Cave Paintings of Baja California'. Mulegé, you know."

"Oh, yes, in that case, Carlos will just love this gift if it talk about those paintings that made him loco. But, Rosa, he loves you much more than he loves any book in the world."

"Yes, Consuelo. I know that. And I am grateful for your tender support since I arrived here. Give me a hug, will you. I love you Consuelo."

Once again, as she had done the first day, Consuelo tightly holds Rosa on her generous bosom. "Do not thank me. Thank the Virgin Mary of Guadalupe, child."

"Yes" answers teary eyed Rosa, "I will."

This time, Consuelo decides to talk straight. She scolds Rosa "Take charge of yourself, kiddo. Enough whimpering. I am the one in charge of the prayers. But you and Carlos … hey? You know what I mean … no? Do not let things drag any longer … hey? For the book, Juanito will take care of the package when it arrives."

—=《》》=—

At night, Rosa decides to not even try Doctor Caldwell's meditation practice. Instead, before going to bed, she goes through a review of her daily achievements and failings. *"You have to admit, Rosa dear, that Carlos manly initiative was wonderful. He really cares for you. You and he are a perfect match. Blessed and encouraged by motherly Consuelo. So, why did you rebuke him when he respectfully suggested going to bed with you? They say that a young girl should say 'no' before saying 'yes'. But there are many ways to say 'no'. After the way you slammed the door in his face with that abrupt 'no' of yours, it's a wonder that he is still courting you. You are not young anymore, Rosa dear. And you and Carlos have been dating for more than a year, now. He wants you. And you want him. So, next time, baby, lean more on the positive side of life, OK? You have only one life. Enjoy it. You already excel in science and business. Time to improve your love life. And by this, I mean your sex life."*

After this personal self-scolding, Rosa instinctively gets on her knees, by her bedside. She has not done that since she was seven, at the time of her first communion. After a short moment, she notices that a Hail Mary has come to her lips, in French. *"Je vous salue, Marie pleine de grâce …"*

Meanwhile, before going to his apartment, Carlos stops in the walk-in freezer to make sure that there will be enough meat and dry supplies while he and Rosa are gone. *"Juanito will have to buy the dairy, vegetables, and fruits … Forget about Juanito, man. Forget about the stupid vegetables. Plan that vacation. She is so sexy. So smart. Gorgeous, really. Man, you must find better approaches to have her come your way. Be more forceful. Not brutal, of course. Forceful, convincing, cajoling. She wants you as much as you want her. No talking needed. Action, man. Action. Do not blame her for saying 'no' the way she did about reserving one instead of two rooms. It's your fault, man. You have to find another, less passive approach."*

Stepping out of the kitchen, Carlos stands a minute in front of the *ofrenda* for a prayer. It is more than a prayer. It is a plea. "God, I beg you. Within the human race you created, help me be a good representative of my extinct Guaycura tribe. Help me be a good life partner for wonderful Rosa whom you have unexpectedly put on my path."

IN LA PAZ AND MULEGE –
Sept 17 to 25, 2015

After the week of touristy fun in La Paz, including one day to visit Sebastian and his delightful wife Margarita, our vacationing pair arrives in the evening at the Mulegé Bed-and-Breakfast. The plan is to take one more day for relaxation and research preparation, before going to the work sites.

Raul and Gina, the elderly owners of the B&B, are delighted to see Carlos who introduces Rosa as his 'lady friend and colleague'.

"Long time no see, Carlos. We were so proud of you, way back when. How long ago? Twenty years?" says Raul who goes on with "You see, Rosa, nowadays we have only tourists. Busloads of tourists. Good money. But not always good company, if you see what I mean. In the old days, Carlos was a first-class guide for professional explorers and researchers of all kinds – biologists, ethnologists, sociologists and what not. I tell you, some of them were well-known professors from all around the world! Things here were much wilder, then, you know. Only dirt roads. No phone, of course. Only brush and rocks, that's all we had."

"And snakes and coyotes, too, I tell you! Is it not so, Carlos?" intones Gina before Raul pleads "Tell us what you remember, Carlos!"

"Yeah, yeah" drawls Carlos.

To encourage Carlos, Rosa joins in the conversation "Oh, yes, Carlos tell us. How did you go from being a guide to an amateur scientist?"

"I was twelve. A good friend of mine is a Cochimi. His Spanish name is Sebastian. He and I were kept at the Todos Santos Mission's orphanage. We did not like it there. He taught me how to speak in his Cochimi language. That way the mean priest could not understand what we said. That would make him mad. To punish us for not talking Spanish, he would beat us and force us to repeat Hail Marys. I did not know any of my own people's language because they were all killed by the white people, you know. One day we ran away. Sebastian had an uncle here in Mulegé. So, we walked all the way. It took us something like a month. Then his family moved to La Paz. One day, some Gringo came and asked me about the local language. So, I translated some words from Cochimi to Spanish. He was happy and paid me good money. And that's it."

Rosa tenderly cajoles Carlos. "Honey, I know that there is more to it than what you just said. Please share the rest of your story with us. What I know of it is beautiful. Tell us some more."

"All right, just because you asked so nicely. Like many kids in underdeveloped countries, I learned to hustle. To eat better, you know. I learned a few words of English. I increased my Cochimi vocabulary asking Sebastian how to say this and this and this, you know. I decided to make a small dictionary with folded paper. The researchers loved that. I did not give them the dictionary, oh no! I asked to be paid for each word they wanted. This way I got good food and bought myself new pants. When I turned fifteen, I told myself. '*I am a Guaycura* Indio *and they want to see* Indios. *I will show them what an Indio can do.*' I started to offer my services as a research guide. Each time a Gringo came, I offered my services. From that point on, I asked them questions and they asked me questions. They liked me for doing that. I asked them if a Guaycura could become a scientist, too. They said yes. They gave me easy-to-read books with pictures. And then I got difficult books. And now twenty years later, I still read new books. People in Todos Santos said I was crazy. I did not care. I wanted to show that Guaycuras are good people. Now, I go on the Internet at the library. I read books written by sixteenth century Spanish Jesuits. They observed and wrote about my ancestors. It breaks my heart to read what they wrote. But it is the only way I can know who my ancestors were and what they did. Until the white men came hundreds of years ago and kill us all. Viciously. Progressively."

"Thank you, Carlos" said Raul. "Your story is wonderful. I did not know about the second part."

"Well. It is not as wonderful as it looks, Raul. I was maturing. As a young man. As a young Indian. The last member of the Guaycura tribe that had been annihilated by white people. I felt like a little monkey at the fair, doing pirouettes to cheer up a new bunch of white people. I became very bitter. That is when I decided to study, study, study to become as smart as those torturing S.O.B.s."

After sharing his introspective comments, Carlos feels embarrassed and nervous. He decides to cut the evening short.

"Good night, friends. Rosa and I will stay here tomorrow to do some work. The day after, we will go to La Trinidad. By the way, Raul, what kind of weather did you have the past few days?"

"Nothing too bad here. But it rained a lot in the San Francisco mountains, as usual."

"After La Trinidad, the day after tomorrow we will go to the Pintas Piedras. I hope that the creek is not too flooded."

"Carlos" interjects Rosa, concerned "would it be dangerous to cross the creek? Because of the rain. As Raul told us. We cannot skip the work at Pintas Piedras. I already have announced it to Professor Harding."

"Do not worry, Rosa. We'll be OK. You can swim some, right?"

"No, honey. I already told you, back home. I can wade in a shallow swimming pool. That's all!"

They turn their respective bedside lights off. Rosa whispers "Carlos, the details you gave tonight about your life, are very touching. They make me love you even more. You were an embittered and pained child. With determination you managed to grow beyond that. Was that not something like a cleansing *limpia*?"

"It was, honey. Thank you for recognizing it. Good night," says Carlos.

"Good night. Sweet dreams."

AT SITE # 1 - LA TRINIDAD – Sept 25, 2015

Carlos and Rosa wake up at the crack of dawn.

They tease each other and giggle like youngsters, for having spent the night in the same room but in separate single beds, as prude college girls would, on their yearly school trip.

"I will carry the equipment bags. Can you take care of the other two?" says Carlos as he walks out of the B&B.

When Rosa arrives at the car, she stops to catch her breath. In awe. Carlos is there, standing straight. In his shorts and sandals. Facing the rising sun, his whole being radiates a glow of primal energy.

She drops her bags to the ground, Carlos approaches her, grabs her around the waist and gives her strong full-body hug. "Again, Rosa, Good morning."

Rosa feels her heart melting. "Good morning, Carlos. You looked so good in the rising sun!"

"I was making the same remark about you, Rosa. But the glowing sun light was around you. Let's go!"

"How far are the caves?"

Carlos takes his tourist guide voice. "Less than twenty miles from here, going Northwest. We will turn right on a dirt road that leads to a ranch. The caves are on the property, one hour hike up the hill from the lodge."

On the way, with Carlos at 'his' Wrangler's wheel, our two explorers go on chatting along.

"Is there a guard at the lodge?"

"The ranch belongs to a doctor. A couple is farming the land. Mostly cattle. They are the ones who take care of the government formalities, collect fees and give instructions to visitors about respecting the site."

"That's a good arrangement, I'd say. Mexico protects its natural environment and archaeological sites better than many other countries."

"That is true, Rosa. But, sad to say, for the past twenty years, real estate development has gone wild, as we saw in La Paz."

The white arrow of a lonely blue road sign points to 'La Trinidad'.

A right turn. They are now on the winding dirt road leading to the ranch.

"In my days, this was a three-foot-wide mule trail. Just enough for a mule and his human companion," jokes Carlos.

They banter back and forth.

Carlos, familiar with all the curves, casually enjoys the Wrangler's features "You know, Rosa, how old fashioned I am about cars. Well, I have to confess something. I did not realize it when we were on the highway, but I absolute love driving this machine on this dirt road. It can handle much rougher terrain. I'd like to find a rough rocky place to try that. Driving this beautiful machine gives such a sense of power. But it is a fake feeling. A feeling that is not rooted in the muscles that God gave me, but in my purchasing power Imagine that. Me, a Guaycura Indian. In 2015. Driving a Sahara Wrangler. It's both weird and wonderful …"

Rosa interrupts, startled. "Did you say 'Sahara'?"

"Yes, Sahara. That's just the car's brand name. So What?"

"Nothing. Nothing." answers Rosa as she quells an electric shock down her spine.

Moody for a moment, she returns to her research notebook. Detailing the impressive landscape. Not as dry as around Todos Santos, the environment is still semi-desertic with lanky cactuses scattered around the scrub vegetation and occasional pine trees.

Awed by the foreboding mountains that surround the valley, she shares: "Those mountains out there are awesome! I never imagined we would see a landscape like this. I wrongly thought that it was kind of flat …"

"Yep! Awesome they are! The land of the Cochimis of old. The land of my Guaycura before the Cochimis. That is where their paintings are, my friend. Be prepared. We'll be walking on those mountains this afternoon."

"You know, Carlos, it's mind-boggling to realize that those high hills and cliffs were formed five million years ago. That's when Baja got separated from the continental mainland. That is why we can see all those cliffs and high mountains."

"You are right, professor. And one day or the other, that will happen around the San Andreas fault in the US. *Adios, San Diego*!"

—=()/()/()=—

"I hope that it does not happen too soon!" concludes Rosa. "Before that happens, I have a question."

"Ask, and I will try to answer" teases Carlos.

"You asked me to wear hiking shoes, long pants and a sun hat. And you are in your sandals, short and no hat …"

Carlos does not let her finish her question. His voice is soft but firm.

"I am a Guaycura, that's why."

After a pause, he continues: "Someday I'll tell you my special philosophy about human feet and footwear. Genuinely derived from Gray's Anatomy …"

—=()/()/()=—

The ranch's small reception foyer has been totally redecorated since the last time Carlos saw it, back in 2005. The tin roof is still there. But some of the cement blocks have been covered with decorative plastic rocks. Beautiful tropical flowers climb on a trellis. The old wooden table and chairs are still there, for the government formalities.

After signing the register, Carlos pulls the Ministry of Archaeology authorization from its shipping tube. As he flattens the document for the clerk, he glances at it and notices the hand-written entry: 'Romero, Carlos. Certified Research Assistant.'

"Rosa! Wow! Thank you. You have entered my name on a Ministry's document ... Me, Carlos the Guaycura. That was very thoughtful, Rosa."

"You certainly deserve having your name there, Carlos. It is natural. You are a Research Assistant. Very few assistants are as knowledgeable as you are."

The clerk launches her sales pitch: "Señora, I'd like to suggest that you get a walking stick. We have them in all sizes and shapes. Twenty pesos for the day. Thirty-five for two days."

"Should I, Carlos?"

"Certainly. I forgot to suggest that, back home. You will find it useful when we get up there."

———⟨ɔ/ɔ/ɔ⟩———

At 8:30, after reserving the ranch guest room for the night, they are ready to go for the hike to site One.

"We'll have to walk a bit faster to make up for time lost. No problem. It is not too far," says Carlos as they leave the gated corral.

"Don't forget to close the gate. They'd be mad if one their cows follows us up the trail!"

"You have a point. Done. But the *charro* [cowboy] who is watching us right now, would not never let his cows develop an interest in painted rocks!"

They take their first steps on the rocky trek. In the fresh morning air, both feel sprite and strong. Carlos takes the lead.

———⟨ɔ/ɔ/ɔ⟩———

The trail is quite steep, from the ranch's valley on up to the tall cliffs partially defaced by erosion. Some of the fallen rocks at the foot of the cliff are covered chunks of paint, like pieces of a gigantic puzzle. Rosa remembers seeing the same kind of eroded rocks elsewhere but does not say anything about it.

Carlos jumps from rock to rock, sure-footed as a Rocky Mountain goat.

Rosa pretends to catch her breath from time to time. Not to rest but to admire her lover's agility. She has gone through many similar expeditions, most of them on equally rough terrains. Never has she seen anybody, including Tuareg shepherds in the Sahara Desert, jump from rock to rock with such nimble manly grace.

Carlos seems to fly from step to step.

Mentally returning to her physics courses, Rosa figures that he uses the kinetic energy from his upper body to move forward.

His feet do not apply a full pressure at each step's point of contact, as most people do. Instead, small directional forces are applied with minute changes in his foot's angular position. Something like steering thrusters on a spacecraft. Or like the intricacy of a bird's feather system as it lands on a tree branch. She secretly delights in watching her lover's athletic exhibition.

———◦/◦/◦———

"Hey, Rosa! Look what you are stepping on!"

"Yes, it's a rock."

"Look carefully at its flat side."

"Oh, yes! I see. This is a segment broken off from the paintings above. Thank you. This is exactly what we want. We can get scrapings off it and get paint samples for dating purposes without having to damage the murals themselves. This is just great. Let's get to work. We have fifty specimen bags. Let's use ten in this area. Here is the routine. You find rocks with paint remainders. I go where you found it, for the photos and the scrapings. We repeat that ten times."

"OK. No problem. And now what?"

"Sorry. Before starting what I just said, without disturbing anything, we identify a rectangular field and take a wide-angle picture of it. For safety, in case of computer problems, I do a paper and pencil sketch. As you go along and successively find the ten painted rocks within that field we go through the identification phase. We ID the piece, pick and brush a few flakes into its small, barcoded plastic bag. I will write everything in the notebook: sketch of the field and pinpoint the location of each specimen. Using the touch screen, I will be able to pinpoint each spot on the field's photo. Oh! I was forgetting. If at all possible, try to find paint chunks of different colors. Tonight, we will clean up the data on the tablet computer."

"That will take a long time, Rosa, no?"

"You are right about that. Let's say … two hours or more for ten bags."

"OK, let's do it. After that we'll move closer to the murals and take our first break there. In time for lunch."

———*✂/✂/✂*———

On the way up to the cave, they stop at the gigantic cactus, one of the La Trinidad site's tourist attractions. They are running a bit late. Yet, they have to comply with the tradition. Posterity will benefit from taking a series of selfies celebrating Rosa-Carlos-in-front-of-the-giant-cactus.

Having lost their walking momentum, they decide to take a short break and eat a bite. Rosa sits on a rock while Carlos, with the giant cactus as a prop, launches a clownish ten-minute presentation about the local vegetation. It is the same ecological speech, memorized word by word in three different languages, that he used to repeat for the tourists of the day.

"'Ladies and Gentlemen. I am now going to tell you about the local vegetation. Starting with this giant cactus. It is a big cactus. That's why it deserves its name of giant. Hahaha!' That, Rosa, used to be the mini-lecture entering statement. To put the visitors at ease, you know. I was saying it in Spanish like right now. Or in English. I did not know a word of English. I was just repeating from automated memory, what one of the researchers had taught me. For some reason, people laughed more at the English version. And each time they gave me a few pesos. I must have been murdering each word, I guess. I tried the same thing for French visitors. But they were stingy. They did not laugh. On the contrary, they seemed to be mad. They never gave me an extra peso tip like the other tourists. So, I stopped telling my gig in French."

"Are you funny! No matter what, dear. The fact that you took this guide job as a pre-teen, showed initiative and your future endurance," remarks Rosa tenderly.

"Yeah, yeah... I will not spend the time now. But my lecture was well organized. I had it mostly memorized. But I had a few notes, too. This way I could meaningfully talk about medicinal plants as used in the old days as well as in modern times like cacti, pinyon trees, mesquite shrubs, junipers, otates, cedros and what not. Oh, I almost forgot. Here are some yellow Damania flowers. They are beautiful in the spring. These are not too wilted. Do you remember, darling?"

"Oh, yes. I will never forget the Damania liquor you offered me in our Cabana Library! I love all you say, Carlos. And I learn a lot."

"When I had time, I used to end the lecture with the story about the Aztec king."

"Tell me more! Now."

"Montezuma, the last Aztec king, was a wise and learned man. In his spare time, he was a botanist. He had a large botanic garden built and maintained to contain samples of all plants growing in his kingdom. When the Spaniards came, instead of benefiting from the scientifically accumulated knowledge, they had the garden destroyed for some religious reasons that I still cannot understand."

———✦✦✦———

They arrive late at the cave. To Rosa's surprise, the cave is just a slight depression into the cliff.

"Sorry to let you know, dear single visitor, a long long time ago, the walls and ceiling of this cave collapsed. Erosion or earthquakes, nobody knows. But the rock paintings at its entrance are exceptional. Most of the caves in the area have impressive paintings for their size and subjects. One can only imagine what these collapsed walls are hiding. So, ladies and gentlemen, put your imagination to work!"

Rosa claps her hands at her lover-guide declamations, while lazily munching on a piece of smoked meat she pulled out of her food bag.

Carlos takes the initiative: "Hey, lady, you seem to be quite hungry. Yet, because we already had a break, I propose that we work first and then have lunch."

"Good plan," admits Rosa while swallowing her last bite. "First let's take photos and some videos. All these artwork pieces have already been documented in many professional and commercial publications. Our job is to take small details about each major piece. Looking at the shape of brush stokes, each engraving, their styles and whether or not different pigments were added over time to underlying designs. When it comes to the specimens, we already used 10 bags. This leaves us 20 for this site and 20 for tomorrow."

"For the record, professor, this place is called the Trinidad Cave. Tomorrow we will be at Pintas Piedras," specifies Carlos.

"Thanks for the info. Let's go to the specimen collection task. Same steps as this morning. Ready?"

"Go!"

Carlos is in charge of the record keeping, this time around.

Rosa, cameras and lens in hand, focuses on the details each main art piece. The deer. The fish. The hunter. The hand imprints (favored by Carlos). The dead steer …

Three hours later they close shop, exhausted.

Carlos decides: "It looks like the weather is turning, Rosa. Let's close shop quickly, have a snack, pack and go. We are lucky."

"Yes? Why is that so?" asks Rosa, full of hope.

"Well. You see, thanks to gravity, the potential energy we accumulated while walking uphill will be returned as we go downhill" answers Carlos in a fake pedantic voice.

CROSSING THE CREEK – Sept 26, 2015

At early dawn, starting for the second site seems to be easier than the previous day.

"Hey, Rosa, don't you feel that your legs and lungs are in better shape today after yesterday's hike?"

"Oh, yes!"

"What should we do when we return home?"

"Let's see. Are you suggesting that we start a daily jogging routine on the beach?"

"You are right, honey. Muscles are made to be used. My ability to walk long distances was a survival asset for my ancestors. The Spanish invaders, and later the curious ethnologists were baffle to see how fast and how long the local bands could go."

"Yes, love, I could not stop admiring that walking gift in you, yesterday."

"What? You were looking at me walk?"

"Yes, and I liked what I was seeing!"

"You know, that is one of the reasons why I got the letter carrier job …"

After passing Site One's cave, the slope becomes steeper and more rocky.

"I am glad you told me to take the walking stick," says Rosa. "Without it, I surely could not walk, here."

Progressively, the trail leads to a canyon. A scary crack in the mountain. Cliffs are covered with wild vegetation, including full trees, crazily hanging, rooted in whatever cracks they could find between the rocky vertical surfaces. The rubble has now been replaced with rounded pebbles laying on top of large, polished areas. At the last zigzag, the canyon has become so narrow that only a sliver of sky can peek between its foreboding walls.

After a last curve, on the other side of a rocky mound, here is the creek, alive. If you listen carefully through the canyon's eery calm, you can hear it. Gently purring yet menacing. Like a mountain lion, quiet but ready to pounce on its prey.

"Our friend Raul was right about raining on the mountains," says Carlos as he takes his shorts and shirt off and sticks them in his waterproof bag. "I will test the waters with my toes, as the expression goes … Hahaha!"

Rosa is amused by Carlos' joke. But her attention is more drawn to his perfectly shaped physique. His tan legs, waist and trunk go progressively deeper into the sparkling water before they emerge, glistening, when he reaches the other bank.

"It is too deep, today." announces Carlos loudly. "I will setup the safety rope. See? On each side, there are deeply anchored iron posts. Super safe. I will string the Ace Hardware rope between the two … You will have to hold the rope tightly with both hands … The current is strong … Do not take your boots off … The pebbles are gone … Taken away by the current … The smooth flat rocks are slippery …"

Back to Rosa, Carlos feels himself in his own element. Elated by the male pride to be responsible for the physical safety of his lover. The crossing will be dangerous, but he is fully confident that it will be alright.

He hands the test bag to Rosa. "Check if it's still dry inside. If OK, I will take the other bags across. Oh, yes! Then it will be your turn, Miss Vasquez! I'll come pick you up. Remember, hold the rope with both hands."

Preparing herself mentally for the plunge, Rosa undresses slowly to her underwear. "Quite a procedure, Mister Romero! Is the water cold?"

"The water? What water are you talking about, miss? Oh, I see. This little stream. One could say that the temp is rather low, yes … that is the case. Lucky you, you will have your dry towel when you get out … I will be behind you honey. No, do not take your shoes off! They will help you on the slippery flat rocks."

⤙ↂↂↂⱻ

Carlos already knew that Rosa had an attractively trim figure for her age. Now crossing the fast current, in the canyon primal intimacy, he allows his eyes to freely focus on his lover's shapely body. And, because of her silence, he knows that she is aware of his visual attentions.

He is glad when they reach the other side. Right behind Rosa in her underwear, ready to hold her in case of slippage, his physical desire was getting too strong …

Rosa gets her towel out of her bag and starts drying herself.

"Carlos dear, would you please dry my back?"

"Of course. Let your boots to dry for a while before we start the climb."

—⋘〇/〇/〇⋙—

Carlos is busy, preparing for the climb to site 2.

Barefooted, Rosa, wading in the creek's edge, takes pictures of the amazing scenery.

"Look at this pebble, Carlos!"

"Honey, I am busy. Yes, I know, there is quite a lot of pebbles around here …"

"Yes, of course. This one is very special. Beautiful. Stuck. I cannot pull it out."

"OK, OK, I'm coming, I'm coming … Oh, my God! This is not a pebble! Let me pull it out …"

"What is it?"

"A turtle shell. A beautiful turtle shell. This is a wonderful omen."

"The turtle shell is a good omen?"

"Yes, of course. I will clean it, keep it in my bag and tell you about it later."

—⋘〇/〇/〇⋙—

Just before taking their first step, Rosa touches Carlos's hand. "For me, crossing the creek, thanks to you and with you, was an experience even more symbolic than the waterfall vision. I do not have enough words to thank you."

Carlos remains silent. Out of respect for the passion of his lover's sincerity.

He takes the first step.

AT SITE # 2 - PINTAS PIEDRAS – Sept 26, 2015

After a while, the slope becomes so steep that, seeing that Rosa is panting, Carlos suggests a short stop.

"Hey," says Rosa "by the way, after the forced bath, I checked all the bags. Not a bit of moisture. The American army sure knows how to make waterproof bags. One wonders why they get rid of them. That's why I was worried when you first talked about it. I thought that army surplus items were nothing but junk."

"I know the background story," ventures Carlos. "Want to hear? Above all, do not leak this info. The US Government has decided to help needy Mexican archaeologists by given them recycled military gear. That's what it is. It is true, I tell you. I read it in the New York Times. Therefore, it's not fake news …"

"Oh, Carlos, you are so funny!"

"Darling, tell me when you have caught your breath. After that, we will climb to the top in a single stretch."

—⟨⟩⟨⟩⟨⟩—

After another steep hike, it is already late afternoon when they reach the Pintas Piedras site. At the top of what could be a volcanic pointed hill, the site is not as complex as site One. But the engravings are much more detailed. Moreover, the site is not covered with chunks of fallen painted rocks.

"You see, Rosa. This site is not as wide. But quite unique, compared to all other ones in the San Francisco Mountains. I noticed it when I was a kid. Because no one wanted to come this high. Since then, I have scoured many publications. I never found it mentioned anywhere in the professional literature."

"Is that so?"

"Yes, this way, Rosa, you will be the first one to analyse it in detail when you publish your article."

"And you will be its co-author, Carlos."

"OK. Let's start. Enough talking, "says Carlos, while springing up to his feet like a Jack-in-the-box. "I am going to show you the most beautiful art piece of all the San Francisco Mountain murals."

Carlos offers an energetic hand to tired Rosa who has a tough time getting up on her own. He grabs her by the waist to give her the little push she needs to walk up the stony slope.

=≈ˢ/ˢ/ˢ=

The superb marine scene is engraved on a 10 by 15 feet slanted pinkish basalt surface. Overhanging as if in a museum, with the dark blue mid-afternoon sky in the background, the prehistoric art piece is breath-taking. All depicted marine creatures are shown in accurate proportions and biological details. Whales in a pod – adults and juveniles - with their fins, blow hole, water jet and barnacled skin. A hammerhead shark. Fish of different sizes. And, strikingly, at the top of the ensemble, a majestic ray.

Stretching herself as high as she can, Rosa absorbs the beauty of the scene, takes pictures of the overall masterpiece before panning on all possible details.

"You are absolutely right, Carlos. We can put this piece in our report, at the center of a picture gallery. Details of the ray are absolutely remarkable. The artist had an incredible eye for proportions. Obviously, he did not bring such a large fish all the way up here, at the top of a cliff, 25 miles from the seashore! Therefore, he accurately drew all those details from memory. Amazing!"

"Right on, Rosa" teases Carlos "no way can anyone carry a ray here. That's even more so for all those whales."

"You do not miss one opportunity to be funny, do you?"

"On a more serious note, Rosa, can you guess why there is a hammerhead shark in the background of the ray?"

"No idea."

"I will tell you. In addition to their graphic art skills, the painters obviously had a precise knowledge of marine biology. A casual observer will just see a hammerhead shark next to a ray. But only an experienced modern biologist will realize that, in their natural habitat, rays are the hammerhead's shark favorite prey!"

Rosa is stunned by Carlos' knowledge. "Where did you learn that?"

"In the National Geographic. That's where. At the Public Library. And remembering this mural, I deducted that those so-called primitive painters might have figured something. For them, this piece was more than a beautiful carving, Rosa."

"Now I understand what you have been telling me, Carlos. In this case, I can visualize the artist. He must have seen his work as the page of an encyclopaedia."

"May I correct you, Rosa? You imply that the artist who created this art piece, thousands of years ago, was a man. I always thought that it was a woman. I even was in love with her when I was a kid …"

"What you are saying might very well be true. It could have been a woman. You are the one who is amazing, Carlos. Very few people … I would say nobody … think the way you do. That is so powerful yet so tender. So human. Obviously, the women of that time might very well have artistic talents, too … That is a wonderful and original thought."

'Oh, come on, Rosa."

"Yes, Carlos. You are strong yet uniquely sensitive."

"Is that because of my Guaycura genes?"

"Most certainly so."

—◁◁◁◁▷—

"OK, Rosa. That's not important for now. Let's go to our work. What will be the sequence this time?"

"We take hi-res pictures. Wide angle then details. After that, we go in the specimen business like before. Twenty more bags. Two for each selected artefact. Detailed ID, as usual. One detailed photo for each spot. In addition, since the site is less trampled and not covered with cave debris, I'd like to take a few organic and inorganic soil samples. From rock crevasses. Unlike caves, too many rains and winds on his hilltop for millenaries."

Just before sunset, the archaeologists are appalled to realize they did not stop to eat.

"We arrived here too late. Our bath party down there, took a long time, remember?"

"If you want to know the truth, I dread going through that again tomorrow."

"It did not rain last night. The level might be lower, tomorrow. But, sorry, you'll have to get wet again. Unless you can walk on water ..."

"Carlos, Carlos, I am going to crack up if you continue with your jokes!"

Evening comes. Carlos-the-guide announces: "Ladies and Gentlemen. Tonight, you will enjoy a paleo dinner. You will eat the same food as the hunter-gatherer people who lived here. Before they became extinct through no fault of their own. While you were admiring their murals, I went in the surrounding nature to collect mesquite wood, gather prickly pears off cacti, pick pinyons from trees and even killed a rabbit. Besides, I packed salted bacalao fish and dried jalapenos in my aloe burlap bag."

To encourage Carlos for his original initiative, Rosa says: "Sounds like a healthy diet. More nourishing than the hot dogs and potato chips that are the favorite food, in so-called advanced societies."

"Right on! Let's start cooking, lady."

Night has fallen. There is a warm southern breeze coming up from the valley below. The moonless sky, not polluted by any city lights, is totally black, letting the stars shine at their natural best. The long-burning mesquite campfire glows in the dark and spreads its wonderful scent.

Carlos has spread dirt and pine needles on a flat rock in front of the campfire. He and Rosa are cuddled under the insulated blanket. Munching on roasted pinyons. Both stay silent, not knowing what to say or do next.

———*()/()/()*———

Carlos makes his move.

Like a virile Guaycura man should.

He sits up, looks at Rosa straight in the face.

"Rosa, I want you to become my wife."

Rosa is stirred. But she immediately answers: "Yes Carlos, I want to be your wife. I have been waiting for you to ask. You are now fulfilling my wish. But first, in fairness to you, I have something to confess. I am not an Argentinian. I am not a Native American. I am a *mestiza*, a mixed blood. North African Berber from my biological father and French from my mother."

"Rosa, I love you. Wherever you came from. I love you for who you are. And, again, I want you to be my wife."

"I too, love you, Carlos. And I want to be your wife."

———*()/()/()*———

After a long kiss, Carlos pulls the blanket over their naked bodies, forgets about stoking the fire and joins Rosa in passionate sex.

———*()/()/()*———

"Carlos, did you feel the earth shaking while we were making love?"

"Yes, many times. That was a terramotto. From our ancestors' souls. Sent from the beyond. To share our pleasure. Here, inside their sacred temple."

Still embraced, they slide into a divine sleep.

117

―――✧/✧/✧――――

The sun is already high in the sky when they wake up. The morning caresses are so tender. Nothing to hurry to. They share tender comments about their lovemaking, whispering in each other's ear.

Carlos teases his lover. "Now we really have fresh news to share with Consuelo."

Rosa giggles "Claro que si, cariño. **On one hand, she might be surprised. On the other, it is likely that she already knows what we did here, last night.**"

"I have a gift for her."

"A gift?"

"A secret. You'll see."

They feel elated, light and youthful as they pack for their return to the ranch where they arrive in mid-afternoon.

―――✧/✧/✧――――

"Were you able to finish you research work?" asks the ranch lady with a mischievous smile.

"Oh, yes. And we had a good time, too!"

"That happens to lots of couples when they come spend time here. I have been told that Mother Nature comes to the help of special people who deserves her goodness."

"Is that so?" kids Carlos, "I did not know. Thanks for telling us."

―――✧/✧/✧――――

Once in Mulegé, they swing by the B&B to say goodbye to Raul and Gina, before hitting the road to Todos Santos.

Their working vacation over, ready to return home, our lovers are both exhausted.

Yet, without having to say a word, they share the soothing feeling of an intimate communion.

Between each other.

With their surroundings.

AT THE ZORRA WATERFALL- Sept 28, 2015

To cover the four-hundred-mile return trip in a single eight-hour stretch, Carlos pushes the Wrangler to the max.

Rosa keeps silent. She dozes off or passively watches the brushy landscapes that pass in front of her weary eyes.

After a rest stop at the Aqua Zarqa restaurant in San Pedro, they are back on the road. A few miles later, Rosa-the-copilot wakes up from her siesta. "Honey, we're on Route 1. Shouldn't we be heading west on Route 19?"

"Good observation. That's because I've got a surprise for you."

"In that case, I'll continue to sleep a while. I love your surprises..."

At La Torré, Carlos leaves caratera 1, turns west, avoids Santiago by turning right, passes over a small river bridge, and continues before arriving at Taqueria la Cascada. It's a nice restaurant, for a well-deserved rest stop. After a good seafood dinner, it takes them only twenty minutes going west to arrive at Rancho Ecologico Sol de Mayo and its large parking lot. The ranch has a very modest lodge. Nothing compared to the one at La Trinidad. But it does its job to guard the entrance of the protected ecological site of the Canyon de la Zorra.

"From here, tomorrow, I'll show you your surprise," says Carlos before signing in for the room booked from Todos Santos.

Rosa watches without a word. She hides an amused smile, thinking: *"Without letting you know, in Todos Santos, for this place, he requested a single room with a single bed ... And now I did not hear you say 'no' ... You have changed a lot since Pintas Piedras, dear Rosa. At last!"* She gives a little caress to Carlos' hand. He responds to her discreet message with a quick smile. "Yes, dear. A good place. And only 4000 pesos, including meals..."

After a light dinner, they go out for a short walk around the parking lot to stretch their legs. It's only 5pm, but the sun has already set behind the Sierra de la Laguna mountains, creating a long, restful twilight. They casually resume the conversations started in Trinidad and Pintas Piedras.

"Hey, Carlos, did you keep the turtle shell I found by the creek?"

"Of course. It is a sacred thing. Full of mythological meaning to us Guaycura and indeed to all Native American nations, wherever they may be on this continent. I cleaned and polished it well. I will give it to Consuelo, according to Guaycura wedding rites."

"Oh yeah? Tell me."

"I'll explain in a few words. The details will come later, next to a brazero at the beach. You must learn and appreciate our mythology. The turtle is a sacred creature. All Native American nations revere it. Because it is the ancestor of the Earth itself. This Earth that we must all respect and protect at all times. The turtle teaches us to live in harmony with humans, animals and all surrounding nature. She is the one who manages the healing, wisdom and spirituality of humans and animals. In addition, my Guaycura ancestors used the shells as vessels for different purposes – from pots to cradles."

"That is a powerful mythology, cariño."

"Yes. There are many others that I will teach you, now that you are my wife.

After a respectful pause, Rosa says: "I have a question, darling."

"Go ahead."

"When did you make the reservation for this room?"

"When, you said? That was in Todos Santos, when we were getting ready ... Why do you ask? ... Oh, I see what you figured out, you smartie lady!"

They kiss and can't stop laughing.

—⟨⟩⟨⟩⟨⟩⟩—

Early, after a good night rest, our couple is having a good time at the ranch's rustic terrace, enjoying a hearty breakfast of chilaquiles.

Rosa can't help but tease Carlos. "You chose a good hotel, sir. Especially the single beds are very comfortable!"

"Ah, you naughty lady, what are you hinting there? OK. Let's get serious now. This morning, before we head back home, I'll take you to see your miraculous waterfall. It's my wedding present to you, Rosa. Just like I promised you on the night of your vision, in April last year. When we were on the other side of this mountain.

"Ah, you went out of your way! So nice of you to do that, my love... One more gift?"

"It's well deserved, you know..."

After twenty minutes, the track's zigs and zags suddenly come to an end, facing a huge scree scattered with wild vegetation. From that point, a steep climb, fortunately equipped with a rope for less gifted climbers - including Rosa -, leads to the site of the waterfall and its wide lagoon.

"See that steep trail there? If we had time, we could go down there. The water is not deep. We could wade to reach and get right under the waterfall."

The view is magnificent. Nature has created a vibrant setting combining raw power and harmonious dimensions. The lagoon is surrounded by a circular cliff of huge polished white rocks covered with daring plants or vines that hang from the top. And in the center of this marvelous jewel box, the waterfall's gem gushes out in a brilliant circle. Like a splashing sun.

Rosa is breathless. She is overcome by a feeling of deep peace.

"That was my vision. Exactly. In every detail. Wonderful."

"Yes, my love, that's why I wanted you to come here."

"But Carlos, tell me how it happened. I was physically with you at the beach in Todos Santos when I first saw it. Exactly as it is before my eyes now..."

"O, woman of little faith! Listen to me, my love. If you understand, your life will open up to a whole new world which, because of your training, you have missed until now. Your being has two components: your physical body and your spiritual soul. Usually, they coexist in what is you. But sometimes, under the influence of good spirits, your soul can step away, come and go, and even wander around. But your body is still alive, mind you. And, when the good spirits so decide, your soul goes back into your body. That's all there is to it. It's simple. It's alright. That's the way it is."

"Yes, now I understand, Carlos. And I believe." whispers Rosa.

"OK, honey. We don't have enough time today. We will come back, some day."

"Oh, yes! Hey, what do you think about coming back here sometime, with Sebastian and his wife Margarita?"

"Great idea. Good ideas are your specialty, dear. Yes, it will be a wonderful time for the four of us."

THE ENGAGEMENT PARTY –
Sept 29, 2015

They arrive at La Linda in mid-afternoon.

Consuelo is – once more – at the front door. As soon as Rosa and Carlos step out of the car, carrying their bags, a whole surprise party crowd flood through the hotel door: Consuelo, of course, Juanito, Carmensita with her white chef hat, and a whole slew of hotel guests … followed by three of Carlos' buddies who happen to be members of a Mariachi band.

In no time, a table is set, loaded with drinks and snacks. Two comfortable armchairs allow the travellers to relax and enjoy the welcome party.

Even before the Mariachis trumpet and guitar have time to start '*Canta no iore*', Consuelo whispers in Rosa's ear: "And sooo?" "Yes," answers Rosa, blushing.

At that very instant, Carlos asks the musicians to hold for a while. He proudly announces: "Hello everybody. We have good news to share with you all. Rosa and I are engaged! And already married, according to the Guaycura tradition. Soon, we will be married, Mexican style."

They all cheer and clap their hands as the *novio* kisses his *novia* passionately.

'*Canta no iore*' starts blaring all over again.

Consuelo manages to dance a few steps, inviting others to follow her lead.

As the party winds down, Juanito takes Carlos aside.

"When you were gone, we received this package. From Amazon. Addressed to you. Here it is."

Carlos opens the package. It's a book about the Baja murals. A collector's edition of 'Cave Paintings of Baja California' by Harry Cosby, with a gift note from Rosa saying: 'To my beloved Carlos, in memory of the beautiful time we had at La Trinidad."

Carlos rushes to the driveway where Rosa is surrounded by partygoers. "Thank you, my love. This is the best gift I have ever received." Then, with his aloe burlap bag in hand, he turns respectfully to Consuelo. Without saying a word, he takes out the turtle shell and offers it ceremoniously to Consuelo. "Rosa found it. On the river's bank."

"¡Qué maravilla! ¡Qué buen augurio!"

"It's a gift for you, Mamma Consuelo. It is the Guaycura tradition."

"Thank you, hijo mio, come with me. Let us put it on the ofrenda, next to the boat."

GUAYCURA SURROGATE MOTHERING – Sept 29, 2015

Evening comes.

Forks in hands, honeymoon couples and other partygoers are lazily settled at the dinner tables.

Tonight, Carmensita and the new *sous-chef* have gone out of their way, for the engagement fiesta. Grouper tacos, the La Linda's signature dish, are the center pieces, surrounded by carnitas and chicken tortilla soup. Beer flows generously. The din becomes so loud that Juanito decides to quell down some of the drunk and over-excited patrons, as it often happens, but usually for the end-of-stay celebrations.

Rosa asks Carlos to step by the poolside. "Could we go down by the beach a while, before the dinner is over?"

"Yes, dear. But what for?"

"I have something important to decide with you."

The partygoers are starting to enjoy Carmensita's desserts with the help of cerveza **or** Damanias

—═⫷/⫸/⫹═—

Our lovers arrive at the beach.

Carlos revives the ambers that still burn at one of the beach fireplaces.

"What I want to say is that, before the trip, I called my doctor in San Diego."

"Your doctor? Something wrong?"

"No, it was my OBGYN. I am not sick. I had a question to ask her."

"I am glad that you are OK, dear. So, what was that question?"

"It's a bit embarrassing."

"Oh, come on … not between us two."

"You know. I am now fifty-four. Way past my child-bearing years."

"Yes?"

"… I asked the doctor if a woman of my age could be a surrogate mother. She said yes, as long as the woman is healthy. When I pressed her to be specific about my personal case, she said that she had already done a number of in-vitro fertilization procedures with a clinic in Los Angeles. They were all successful. The candidate surrogate mother must not be overweight. There should not be any diabetes, blood anomalies nor any heart problem."

"Thank you for those medical details, honey. But what is your point?"

"Well … she said that I was healthy enough. She said that I am a good candidate."

"A good candidate for what?"

"Let me phrase it right, honey. Many times, you have said that you regretted not having any Guaycura children of your own."

"Oh Lord! I now know what you are going to say! Rosa! Rosa!" says Carlos, shaken, his eyes tearing.

Rosa remains silent, herself holding a profound sob.

Concerned, Carlos returns to the tense conversation. "I want to hear more. Can there be complications for such a mother?"

"Yes, of course. But the doctor is convinced that all the conditions are positive, based on my last exams and my general health. Any difficulty can be handled without major problems, as long as the procedures are carefully followed. She has had many successful cases."

"I have to confess, Rosa. Right now, I cannot possibly be my macho self. Your plan, so thoughtful, so generous, is shaking me… I cannot fathom the depth of your love … So profound … So unique …"

Carlos stops talking. He cannot hold his tears, as Rosa silently holds his hands.

"How is that done, since you cannot get pregnant?"

Rosa pauses before starting to explain the details: "The clinic performs an in-vitro procedure. Your sperm is used to fertilize a woman's eggs that are then inserted in my womb. I then carry the baby normally. This is really the easiest part."

"I am baffled. Who would that woman be? "

"Margarita, Sebastian's wife," answers Rosa calmly. "I asked her. She agreed. And so did Sebastian."

"What?"

"Yes, our baby will be half Guaycura and half Cochimi."

"Rosa, oh, Rosa. You really are an angel. My angel."

PLANNING THE LIMPIA – Sept 30, 2015

The day after the engagement party, Consuelo asks Carlos to come to her apartment.

"Carlos, I have to tell you. This morning, Don Pedro said that the good spirits are ready for the Rosa's *limpia* …"

Carlos interrupts to take charge of the conversation. He is the novio. He is the one who must decide.

"The September full moon is tomorrow. No time to get ready. So, it will be on October 26th. Rosa is calm after the good time we had on the vacation. The engagement and the party gave her a new boost. She is happy to see that business is running well. We will have a full month for our spiritual preparation. But the treatment will have to end before the Day of the Dead, on the 31st."

"Well, so be it, Carlos. She is your *novia*. Your decision is the best. Don Pedro said it will be a special *limpia espirituale*. We must not force. Let the good spirits work. It will take one or many nights. Depending on whether the bad spirits get out of her body right away or not. Don Pedro told me the potions to fix. The herbs to burn. Some weak, some strong, you know. Peyote tea. Coca leaves. You know. So, she sleeps and then not sleep. Perhaps she sleeps in the day and become half-awake in the evening. Then she cannot stop talking and talking all night."

"All night, you said?"

"Yes. All night long. You don't understand, or what? And you stay next to her and write down what she says. I cannot write you know. I can remember most everything, but I cannot write. So, you are the one who writes. At night you start with one question. You say 'What is your name?' This is for the good spirits. So they know to get prepared to chase the bad spirits. And then you say 'What are you going to tell us tonight?' This is to scare the bad spirits. So, do you understand, or you do not understand?"

"Yes, I understand, Consuelo." Somewhat irked, Carlos finishes to write down the instructions in his study notebook. "I will do that. She is my *novia*, now. I will take good care of her. Just like you tell me."

"Don Pedro said, after the bad spirits get out of her, then she will be free for the rest of her life. And that the both of you will be happy."

"That is what I want for her. To be happy the rest of our lives. Together."

"That's good, my child," concludes Consuelo. But she cannot stop her matchmaker routine. "So, what do you do for a whole month until the *Limpia*? You are the *novio* and she is the *novia*. You two know what has to be done, no? Or do you want me to explain?"

This time, the rubbing is too strong for Carlos. After a stiff silence he goes on bitterly: "I know, Consuelo. I know what to do ... I do not need an instructor to court Rosa."

Realizing that he is better off showing respect Consuelo than dwell on his own anger, he goes on, with a respectful smile: "But, Consuelo ..."

"Yes?"

"... I understood all the instructions you gave me. I wrote them down in this notebook, see? Before and after the *limpia*, Rosa and I will share our lives. And all of that thanks to you, mama Consuelo."

"¡ Suerte. Lo sé que todo salga bien!"

[Good luck. I knew everything would be alright!]

Right after leaving Consuelo's apartment, Carlos knocks at Rosa's door: "Honey, I have good news for the both of us."

"I like good news, especially the ones that come from you, honey."

"First, Don Pedro has decided that your *limpia* will be on the October's full moon."

"What day will that be?"

"The 26th or the 27th."

"Then what, Carlos?"

"Well, the *limpia* will last many nights. Until you are cured, dear."

"Many nights? How many?"

"I have no idea, honey. Two, three? Maybe more. I do not know. It will be as needed. That's all."

"Many nights, hey? Like Shahrazad?"

"Shahrazad? Who is Shahrazad? I am getting confused" admits Carlos.

"Oh, it's a story. No big deal. I'll tell you later."

"Whatever … Don Pedro also said that, between now and then, you should take it easy. Not to worry about the hotel. Just do what you like."

"I hear you. But does Don Pedro know that what I like most is to be with you?"

"I am sure that he knows that. If the idea escaped him in view of his age, I imagine that Consuelo has already refreshed his memory!"

"Don Pedro did not say anything against wedding plans, did he?"

"Nope. Neither did he discourage us against planning our honeymoon!"

"OK. Therefore, for one more month, we forget about La Linda. We relax. But at the same time, you take the lead for the honeymoon plans. I manage wedding preparations, with Consuelo's and Carmensita's help."

"Rosa, Rosa, what about all the research work we have to do? Organizing, documenting, and writing about our findings at La Trinidad and Pintas Piedras. Remember, Rosa, that you must submit the expedition's results this coming January."

"You are definitely right. Love made me forget all about work … Thanks a lot for reminding me! What is best for the research work? Mornings or afternoons?"

"I'd say mornings. Right after an early breakfast."

"That's a deal!"

"Not yet! Do you remember our resolution at Pintas Piedras? We decided then, to keep in shape by jogging on the beach each morning. Barefooted!

In the evening, time at the beach: munching roasted pinyons, in front of the campfire."

"Something like we did at Pintas Piedras?" flirts Rosa.

"Yes, something like that."

All smiles, Carlos grabs his lover by the waist and gives her a long kiss.

She returns it passionately.

MIDDLE-AGED LOVERS –
Sept 30 to Oct 26, 2015

As expected, Rosa and Carlos happily agreed to comply with Don Pedro's shaman therapy plan.

To be best prepared for Rosa's limpia catharsis, they both took a month off. Consuelo and Carmensita are in charge of the hotel.

But there is plenty else for them to do.

Working in the La Linda Research Library, our two lover-archaeologists use their time to relaxedly process the expeditions field data.

And to reflect about their lives.

Past and future.

It is almost two years ago that they met, thanks to Consuelo's intervention. They soon realized that through their interest in archaeology, they could get to know each other better. At first, they never thought that their common interest would lead them to love and passion. Now they have no hesitation: they enjoy each other's company. The time has come to anchor these budding feelings in immediate reality, through personal and mutual enrichment efforts.

Every moment, every action is reason enough to express their pent-up passion: sweet words, gestures, hugs and kisses.

On the other hand, their enthusiasm for science encourages them to organize and plan their activities. Some might think they are too compulsive. But they have a goal in mind: no longer in their prime years, they want to accomplish several focused goals. Together. For the rest of their lives.

Rosa had the idea to share and write down their values and aspirations. It will be a document of their life journey together and will define a roadmap for their married life.

After years of severe romantic drought, they discovered the innocent happiness experienced by most people in their twenties. The delay is only a minor handicap. They counterbalance it with a middle-aged sense of gravitas. This gives them deep satisfactions that young people cannot experience!

As mature lovers, they know they are taking the most important step in their lives. To give meaning and define achievable life goals, they engage in open communication in a spirit of respect and mutual support.

They realize the uniqueness of their experience. Coming from radically different cultural backgrounds, they are now able to achieve happiness at the crossroads of their emotional journey.

—=⟨⟨⟨⟩⟩⟩=—

Rosa takes the lead.

"Carlos, my love. I have evolved a lot since I arrived in Todos Santos two years ago. And especially since we met and fell in love."

"You are right about that, *cariña*. And it has been a pleasure for me, I assure you."

"All my life, I have been striving to excel in scientific work. I managed to achieve a lot in the fields that captured my passion. People admired me. But I did not know how to be loved … until I met you. Then, the western-trained scientist part of me was traumatized by the side-effects of a world gone crazy. Thanks to you, Carlos, I have found peace by embracing the mysticism aspects of your society."

"You say things so nicely, dear. On top of that, your comments have a profound meaning. Tell me. I do not want to be intrusive, but what were those traumas that hurt you so deeply?"

"Oh, it was nothing. Nothing worth talking about. OK, I told you about myself. Now it's your turn!"

—=⟨⟨⟨⟩⟩⟩=—

"My turn? You want me to talk about myself? Rosa, I have no idea where to start!"

"Well, you can start talking about the feelings you had during your childhood. You described them so deeply when we spent that nice evening at Raul's and Gina's in Mulegé."

"Thanks for putting me on the right track, Rosa. Who am I? Well, I am the last embittered member of a 'primitive' ethnic group victim of a western-led genocide. I have been traumatized. But my personal traumas pale in comparison to the atrocious pain experienced by my relatives and ancestors. Strangely, I feel their pains more intensely than mine. I imagine that it is the same raw pain experienced by all victims of colonial oppression. By all the victims of racism, wherever it shows its ugly head. Do you see what I mean?"

"Yes, I do, Carlos. Not as sharply as in your case. But I do see. Through my Berber connection."

"What connection are you talking about?"

Rosa is once more caught short. "Oh, nothing, nothing."

"Whatever that connection may be, I can say that, thanks to you, thanks to the relationship we have developed, thanks to our love, I have come to realize that my self-pitying bitterness is devoid of any purpose. I was studying ethnology with a vengeance. To prove that my 'primitive' qualities are not an obstacle to reaching the heights of human achievements. Progressively, it has dawned on me that 'primitive' people possess qualities that failing western societies must now re-learn. Therefore, there is absolutely nothing in me, or in any other Native American, that can be classified as primitive or inferior to anyone else in the world."

"Right on, Carlos. Love has brought us together. We come from opposite ends of the human experience. Do you feel like I do? Don't you think that you and I are entering a new era that will blend intellectual prowess and wholesome spirituality?"

"Yes, Rosa. You said it right. For now I want to celebrate with a good hug …"

"That's fine by me. Let's do it!"

135

CHAPTER 2

Transcription of the notes taken by Carlos during the four nights of psychotherapy treatment.

PREPARING FOR THE LIMPIA – Oct 26, 2015

Rosa's *limpia* will start tonight, as planned. It might take one or more nights. The timing is perfect. Hopefully, the *limpia* will be over right before the Dia del Muertos festivities when, traditionally, the whole town celebrates, in the company of the departed.

Working as a team, each of the four friends (Don Pedro, Consuelo, Carlos, and Rosa) knows his or her role to expel the demons. They will rid her of those hidden bad spirits that have invaded her for some strange reason.

Using his traditional therapies, Don Pedro hopes that Rosa, under induced hypnosis, will share her repressed negative memories. He knows that once drugged, Rosa will talk about her past. A tunnel will form between her soul and the outside world. Through it, the bad spirits that invaded her during an unknown traumatic event, will be expelled. Rosa will then be healed.

Consuelo will be Don Pedro's assistant. Each day, as instructed, she will prepare pre-dosed potions, some including magic mushrooms; and burn aromatic herb bundles to alternatively sedate and then stimulate Rosa. Starting in the early evening, she will give the patient secret medications of increasing concentrations. Those will put Rosa enter into night-long hypnotic trances. Her inhibitions that have been blocking her will collapse. Miraculously, tell-all monologues about her life and traumas will expel the bad spirits.

Carlos, as Rosa's *novio*, will give her loving support during the day. At night, he will be at her bedside. He respects Don Pedro's mysticism. He saw many people cured by him. On the other hand, as a self-trained scientist, he values the obvious merits of modern psychiatry. His role will be to run a tape recorder and take detailed notes of what Rosa says during her nightly induced hypnosis. The following morning, he will share those notes with Don Pedro who, in turn, will adjust the following night's treatment, as needed.

Their love is what makes Rosa have faith in her own recovery.

For her, it will be a born-again experience.

She is ready.

NIGHT # 1 – Oct 26, 2015 – BEFORE THE TERRORIST ATTACK

A strange yet profoundly touching treatment is going to start. A catharsis performed, not as a one-on-one session with the therapist, but involving family members, according to the instructions given by Don Pedro, the curandero.

The catharsis will be done in Consuelo modest house in the Cabessa Blanca neighborhood, not far from Don Pedro's clinic. She has setup a special corner in the living room. Using a white sheet and a rod, Carlos has built a makeshift partition to isolate the *ofrenda* from the treatment bed. The departed must absolutely not be disturbed.

After sunset, Carlos leads Rosa to her treatment bed. Using smoke and secret potions, Consuelo will continue to condition Rosa into a hypnotic trance. Carlos is at her bedside, the tape recorder ready to start. Hypnotized, Rosa starts a long monolog, interrupted only by Consuelo's increasingly powerful potions. At times, Rosa is rambling. At other times she is clear as a bell. Carlos takes notes about the patient's behavior and write down clarifications as needed. Tomorrow, he will deliver the session's audio tape and notes to Don Pedro.

"What is your name, dear. And what do you want to tell us tonight?" says Carlos, according to the prescribed ritual.

"My name is Rosa. Rosa Vasquez."

"I was born and lived in a mixed-up world.

Few people around here know about that world.

All kind of things happened to me before I ran away to Baja.

I was running away from pain.

My mom is dead. Her name was Mary Blanchard.

She was always a good mother to me.

Loving, caring, doing her best. She had a tough life.

I loved her. I love her now and always will.

She is my hero and my role model.

She never gave up and was always true to herself.

Burdened by shame and guilt, she seldom shared anything about herself.

For many years, I asked her childish questions.

Then I grew up.

By dribs and drabs, I figured what her life had been.

—⟨♪/♪/♪⟩—

My mom was American. Born in 1938. In a small farming village of Central Ohio.

The only child of a conservative Mennonite family of French origin.

Isolated, she loved to write to a cousin of hers, who was living near Paris.

—⟨♪/♪/♪⟩—

My mom liked to talk to me was about her first marriage.

Right after graduation in 1956, she married Vyktor, her high school sweetheart.

Vyktor Rheinhart was not good at anything. But he could pump iron. Unable to get a regular job, he was giving muscle exhibitions at surrounding villages.

To make a better living, the young couple decided to hitchhike throughout the Midwest. Looking to be hired for wrestling contests at saloons and county fairs. For five dollars a bout. One dollar tip if there was lots of blood.

One day, in Milwaukee, he lucked out. A Hollywood scout spotted him. They were finally happy. They settled in a glitzy Los Angeles neighborhood.

He got minor roles in B-rated movies.

Thanks to his sexy shape and bulging muscles, he was popular among teenage girls.

Followed by groupies, Vyktor thought he had made it. Sudden riches and popularity were followed by drug habits. Vyktor changed to the worst but continued to make lots of money.

—————

My mom was disgusted. Her Christian faith meant a lot to her.

She asked for a divorce in 1960.

Proud, she refused to accept any alimony on religious principles.

She ran away to France. Her hope was to first live with her cousin.

And from there, she was hoping to find some way to make a living on her own.

Bad luck hit her again.

One week after she arrived, her cousin died in a car accident.

She found herself with no money. No connections. No Mennonite Church. Not able to speak French.

But still gutsy.

She got a job as a hotel maid in Barbès.

That is a seedy North African immigrant neighborhood in Paris.

—————

Tarik, a Berber Algerian student in archaeology at the Sorbonne, was the night receptionist at that hotel.

He was charming and good looking.

My mom and he fell in love. They dated.

They spent weekends at his Algerian buddies in the students' Quartier Latin of Paris.

At that time, there were political troubles in France.

My mom knew that there was a war in then French-occupied Algeria.

But she did not care too much about politics.

Tarik was an Algerian patriot. He had joined the anti-colonialist movement.

A year before I was born, they decided to live together.

In her apartment.

So Tarik could hide from the French police.

On October 17th, 1961, Tarik joined a peaceful march of Algerian protesters.

The march was blocked on a bridge.

Close to Notre Dame Cathedral.

Maurice Papon, then prefect of police or Paris, had given orders to hit hard.

A few hundred Algerian marchers were killed.

To give a lasting example to the would-be protesters, the police lobbed bodies over the bridge into the Seine River.

That is how Tarik, my biological father, died.

I was born a week later.

⸺ひ/ひ/ひ⸺

Until age seven, I was called Rose Blanchard. The daughter of a destitute single mother. Life was good, though. I loved my mom and she loved me. She was mine. Not to be shared with anyone else.

Poor and fatherless, I was the target of bullies. At school, I was bullied for being an Arab. In the Barbès neighborhood, I was bullied for being French.

But I did not mind, thanks to my mom's support. At five, I decided to become as strong as she was.

Always tough.

Always hopeful.

———❦———

On my seventh birthday, Mom served ice cream and cake. "Lovely Face, here is your birthday present. Open it. I loved your daddy before he died. He would have loved you too. He gave me this book. Now I am giving it to you. Happy birthday, my darling!"

I could not understand why she was crying. The book had delicately decorated pages.

"Honey, this book is called the 'Arabian Nights'. Another name is "The Tale of One Thousand and One night." It is about a young gutsy lady, called Shahrazad. Like you, Lovely Face! Read it many times as you grow up."

'Lovely Face'.

I liked the sound of that nickname! I loved it so much that Mummy wrote it in a small locket she gave me. I still have it.

"Your daddy told me that he was a Berber. He was from the village of Aït Wufur, in Kabylia. He wanted you to know that. He died right before you arrived from heaven. You must know about your daddy. Love him. As he loved you before you were born."

———❦———

From that day on, I looked for Tarik, my Berber dad. He was alive, in my head and my heart.

That was the only thing that counted.

I was proud to be a Berber, just like my daddy.

I decided to become a student, just like him.

Right after the seventh birthday party, my mom decided to re-marry.

She told me that she was getting too old and worn out to go on doing maid work.

Her new husband was a widower with two daughters of his own. He was a survivor of the 1930s Spanish Civil War. Turned Pied-Noir he was one of the million European settlers who fled Algeria in 1962. His name was Paolo Vasquez. He moved us from Barbès to his small house in the Paris *'banlieue'* [suburbs].

Paolo hated me.

He wanted to get rid of me because I was a 'no-good Berber monkey'. My mom said that he had to adopt me. That's how my name was changed from Rose Blanchard to Rosa Vasquez.

Mother and I were forced to speak Spanish at home, even though he was practically illiterate. We were punished if he or his daughters would catch us speaking French.

To be ornery, I took Spanish in school. I became fluent in Castilian Spanish. That made Paolo mad. I had him beaten!

My half-sisters were taunting me non-stop.

Paolo was a drunk. And a racist.

He called me his 'dirty Arab thing'. Even when he was trying to be nice during his filthy sexual advances.

144

I braced myself.

I remained true to myself.

I refused to flinch.

I refused to give up.

I escaped through studies. To be the best student I could be. In all subjects. Especially in sciences.

I learned English too. That was easy. It felt secretly good to know that 'Lovely Face' was an English nickname.

That's how got my PhD at the Sorbonne. In ethnology. At 18.

I chose archaeology.

Just like my daddy wanted before he was killed by the French police.

To know about my father's Berber people, I got a job with an immigrant support agency in Paris. The pay was low. But I loved it.

I helped immigrant Algerian women adapt to life in France. Most of them were Berbers. It was perfect for me. I progressively learn algerian Arabic and the Berber language to be able to converse with my clients.

I went crazy studying Berbers. Everything about Berbers. Their family life, recipes, language, ancestral tales, religion, history. Wherever they were. From the Canary Islands to Morocco, Algeria, Tunisia, Libya, Egypt, to the Sahara Touaregs. I learned that all Algerians are from Berber descent. But some tribes have joined the Arab civilization, while others – mostly the Kabyles like my dad– kept their ancestral language and culture, even though they are Muslims.

I wrote articles about Berbers in women's magazines.

And in professional ethnology publications.

I was looking for a father.

I discovered a whole civilization.

—————

My mom died.

My only support.

I was heart-broken.

To know my father's country, at twenty-one in 1982, I got a job as assistant research professor at the University of Algiers. In the Department of National Antiquities.

My first project was to recreate the documents and books lost after the bombing and fire by the by Pieds-Noirs terrorist Secret Army Organization in 1962.

To feel even more in contact with dad's world, I asked to get the Algerian citizenship. I was surprised to get it in no time. As if I had some support from the government.

They changed my legal first name to Ourida, which means Rose in Arabic, but I continued to be called Rosa.

That is when the terrible Black Decade civil war started with its hundreds of thousands of dead.

Life there became crazier and crazier.

Algerian terrorists pledged allegiance to Bin Laden's Qaeda. Contained in the north, they moved to the Sahara. Where the rock paintings are. I had to continue my research work. To inventory all rock paintings in Algeria. Despite the insecurity.

—————

My last expedition before early retirement was in January 2013.

To the Tassili N'Ajjer Mountains.

On the way back from that site, we were attacked by terrorists."

—⟨∘∕∘∕∘⟩—

One full hour has gone by. Consuelo decides that 'it's enough for the night' and gives Rosa a spoonful of a strong soporific syrup. Carlos turns the tape recorder off and organizes his notes. Consuelo and Carlos know that they are not allowed to talk about what they heard from Rosa: the spirits must not be disturbed. Only Don Pedro is allowed to diagnose. Otherwise, the charm would be broken. But they have privately learned a lot about their dear friend.

NIGHT # 2 – Oct 27, 2015 –
THE FAKE CHECKPOINT

After a day of total bed rest, Rosa is returned to the improvised treatment room, for her second nightly catharsis. Consuelo and Carlos prepare for a repeat of the first night's ritual.

———❦❦❦———

"What is your name, dear. And what do you want to tell us tonight?" says Carlos, according to the prescribed ritual.

"My name is Rosa. Rosa Vasquez."

———❦❦❦———

"Until two years ago, in 2013, I was Director of National Antiquities at the University of Algiers. In charge of prehistoric rock paintings in the Sahara Desert.

The terrible Black Decade civil war was going on in Algeria. I got engaged to Arezki. He was professor of French Lit. We lived in a little apartment next to a park, up the street from the university. We were planning to get married. He took me to visit his folks in the small village of Mekla.

I asked Arezki to take me to the village of Aït Wufur.

Where my dad Tarik was born.

Hoping to finally trace him.

I was terribly disappointed. And scared.

Some villagers knew of him.

But nobody wanted to talk about him.

Three months later Arezki was killed by terrorists. Right in front of our apartment building. Just because he spoke French and not Arabic.

Or, as secretly suggested by a university friend, he might have been killed for having asked too many questions about my dad when we went to Aït Wufur.

I was shattered. What were the abject reasons for my sweet Arezki's murder? How could there be a link between my fiancé's death and my dad's life in Aït Wufur? My life became unbearable. Was I going to be targeted in this atrocious civil war where anyone could either be a criminal or soon become the victim of a crime? I escaped into obsessive work.

———✄✄✄———

Until the end of the Black Decade in 2001, for safety and to overcome by paranoia, I stopped staying at my apartment. I setup a mattress bed in an office corner and got my meals out of the campus vending machines, while terrorism and counterterrorism were raging around.

———✄✄✄———

The last expedition before my early retirement in 2013 was to specific rock paintings at Tassili N'Ajjer in the Sahara Desert. At that location, there are lots of paintings and engravings over 30,000 square miles. They show climatic changes, animal migrations and the evolution of human life.

There were four of us. Two young Algerian PhD students, myself and a young British lady. She thought we were a tourist agency.

I feel terribly guilty for letting her join us.

Just like many others, her British oil-executive dad had shady connections with Sonatrach, the Algerian state oil company.

I was forced to take her with us on the expedition.

Here we were. Three crazy archaeologists and one air-headed British kid. Looking like happy tourists.

We fell in a snake pit.

———✄✄✄———

We left on January 5. In the morning. From the Boufarik airfield military airport. On a Russian Ilyushin Il-76 military transport plane. With servicemen families. To Tamanrasset, the capital of the Tuareg Berbers, in the middle of southern Sahara. We arrived there 3 hours later. And stayed at the Tahat Hotel.

The students and the Brit girl were scared by the heavy military presence.

———<(/)/)/)>———

The next morning, on January 6, a Russian-built all-terrain TIGR military vehicle was ready for us. For an 18-hour trip on route N5 to the Tassili Cultural Park Office in Djanet.

For security we were assigned to an official guide driving the park's Jeep, accompanied by an Algerian army military escort. The army lieutenant in charge of us confided that satellite photos were showing suspicious activity East of the nearby Libyan border.

The rock art dating work of some pieces from the so-called 'Horse Period' was easy. We were finished in 4 days, ready to return to Tamanrasset and catch our flight back to Algiers.

Instead, we got a call. "Your return flight from Tamanrasset had been cancelled … You will leave from the In Amenas airfield … Government big shots and foreign business executives are coming from Algiers to visit the gas plant. They will stay at Hotel Tayat before going to In Amenas. You must leave the hotel today."

Our guide talked about rumors. Security was tighter than ever before.

The TIGR picked us up late.

At around 3 in the afternoon.

Ahmed, the driver was a friendly and talkative Algerian sergeant who knew a thing or two about terrorists.

On the front passenger seat, two machine guns with their ammo strips made us feel safe.

We were all tense, crammed in the low-roof army TIGR.

We tried to stay in good spirits.

Talking about work issues and what not.

To spend time and forget our fears.

The N3 road to Zar Zaitine-In Amenas airport goes straight up North.

Nothing to see except the horizon.

⎯⎯⟨∂/∂/∂⟩⎯⎯

It is getting dark.

We arrive at a big curve in the road, not far from In Amenas.

Standing alone in the middle of the road, what looks like an Algerian army officer signals us to stop, waving a red flashlight.

Friendly. Polite. He asks in French: "Thank you for stopping. Please step out for a short while."

We step out of the TIGR.

Happy to shake our legs. Expecting just a routine check.

Three terrorist militants jumped from the dark. Out of a Toyota 4by4 that was hidden behind a dune.

They, and the fake officer jump on us all, including Ahmed, our driver.

The terrorists are efficient and coordinated.

They say nothing, make no sound.

Within a few seconds, we are all face down in the rocky sand. Feet bound and hands behind our back, held with plastic ties.

Like mindless robots, the three militants run back to the Toyota.

It was like the Black Decade 'faux-barrage'. The GIA terrorists specialty. Wearing stolen uniforms, the terrorists would stop civilian vehicles. and process their passengers as needed. Kill or kidnap them for ransom.

The fake officer shouts an order.

The three militants return. Take our research bins, our suitcases. And the machine guns and the ammos from the TIGR.

The fake officer comes to each of us. Searches our pockets. Verifies and keeps all ID documents.

He announces: "We do not hurt our civilian Muslim brethren. We only get rid of the vermin. We kill only the military and miscreant foreigners."

He unties my hands. And shouts in Arabic: "You, filthy whore. We give you one chance. If we found you not wearing a veil, you are dead. Like a rotten foreigner."

He unties the students' feet. Two militants lead them to the 4by4.

The brave captain points his gun to the British girl's head. She cries. Asks for pity.

I scream: "No! No! No!"

"Shut up, whore. Unless you want to join the foreign bitch in hell."

He pulled the trigger.

The body arched backward in a last convulsion.

He then went to coldly shoot Ahmed the driver.

Twice.

After a few steps towards the 4by4, pushed on his remote-control detonator.

The TIGR goes up in flames.

The bastard then goes on his way.

Against the night's total desert blackness, his silhouette is lit by the horrid red bulb of the burning TIGR.

The blast pushed me some ten feet away.

Using my freed hands, I repositioned myself. I got on my back.

Once the TIGR fire went off, I could see the immensity of the Saharan night sky.

I did not know that something had happened. I did not even think about untying my feet. I collapsed into a sick torpor.

—=∙∙(∙/∙/∙)∙=—

I regained consciousness. I know I am in a hospital bed. At the In Amenas natural gas plant clinic.

A large red-faced fellow was talking to me.

In English. I know he is a medic.

"Good morning, Lovely Face!"

—=∙∙(∙/∙/∙)∙=—

I felt myself shaking my head.

'Lovely Face'.

My English nickname. From my mom.

'Lovely Face'. The talisman. She wrote it on a piece of paper. In my plastic locket.

When I was so tiny.

So tiny.

—=∙∙(∙/∙/∙)∙=—

"My name is Jim. What is your name?"

I wanted to talk. But I did not even think of moving my lips.

Everything looked flat.

Flat, flat, flat.

Like a gigantic painting without edges.

—◦/◦/◦—

This time, two hours have gone by. Consuelo realizes that the catharsis session has gone for too long. Rosa is obviously exhausted and distraught. She gulps her spoon of soporific syrup. Carlos turns the tape recorder off and organizes his notes. Consuelo and Carlos know that they are not allowed to talk about what they heard from Rosa: the spirits would be disturbed. Only Don Pedro is allowed to give a diagnostic. Otherwise, the charm would be broken. But they are privately appalled to now know that the bad spirits invaded Rosa's soul during that horrible terrorist event on the Saharan road.

NIGHT # 3 – Oct 28, 2015 – THE TERRORIST ATTACK

After a day of total bed rest, Rosa is returned to the treatment room, for her third nightly catharsis. Consuelo and Carlos now know the routine. They know that Don Pedro has told them to not exchange a word about Rosa condition. Yet, they are both silently anxious to know more about the terrible ordeals that their dear friend has gone through in the far away African desert. At the hand of viciously crafty terrorists.

"What is your name, dear. And what do you want to tell us tonight?" says Carlos, according to the prescribed ritual.

"My name is Rosa. Rosa Vasquez."

"The flat red face is talking to me in French and in English.

I cannot talk.

But can hear him.

I understand most everything he says.

"My name is Jim. Je suis Americain."

"Your name? What country?"

Everything is flat. Flat, flat, flat. Like a huge painting without edges.

I want to talk but have no voice.

My head is empty of any word.

He gives me pills. He is taking good care of me. I know he is a medic. I know I am in a hospital bed.

He asks many times: "What's your name?"

I do not know my name.

"OK, lady. That's OK. Don't tell me your name. I will call you Lovely Face."

He saw me wiggle in the bed.

My nickname. Lovely Face.

When I was tiny, Mom called me Lovely Face.

When I was so tiny.

So tiny.

"Hey, look at your lovely face in the mirror."

"Maybe it will help you remember who you are."

He puts the hand mirror right against my nose.

I want to scream. Open my mouth wide. But no sound.

I hate that. I hate my face. I hate myself. I hate Jim. I hate my life.

—=✿✿✿=—

Other men came. Some Algerians. Some foreigners. All were flat.

They were talking to Jim. They were all upset.

"Who is she? Her name? What did she say? Coming from where?"

Jim says :"The employee bus picked her up this morning. At 5. At the big curve. Two dead."

They talked to me mad. In French and in Arabic.

"Who was with you?"

"Who was the young lady?"

"Why they killed her and did not kill you?"

They talked about me. "Why don't you want to give your name?

Were you with the terrorists? Where are your papers?"

They talked about the fake checkpoint.

I could only stare, not moving, not talking.

Then the men left.

One night went by.

—⟨)/)/)⟩—

All day Jim played a song on a boombox.

A CD. Always the same song. Again, and again.

"Hotel California," he said.

I started to know some of the words.

"Hey, Lovely Face. Do you like this song? From the good old USA.

"Listen to it. It will do you good."

Played it again and again.

The song reshaped my insides.

Things were getting less flat.

I was finding reality again.

Nothing else happened that day.

One night went by, again.

—⟨)/)/)⟩—

Early morning arrived with noises.

Machine guns, screams, explosions.

Then the long siren.

Jim screamed: "Lock down!"

Silence.

Then gunshots.

Silence.

Then loud explosions.

I started shaking.

Jim made me drink and take pills.

Took me to the bathroom to pee.

Then pushed me in a closet. With a blanket. And a water bottle.

Outside gunshots and explosions.

I kind of did not care.

All day.

Then there was a big bang.

The trailer rattled.

Jim screamed.

—=✧✧✧=—

From inside the closet, I can hear commotion in the infirmary. Noises of fighting.

Angry men in funky battle dress rip my closet door and drag me out.

I know they are terrorists. Same uniform as that night on the road.

They scream in Arabic: "You, you are whore of a foreigner? Get out or we'll kill you."

Jim rush to protect me.

They shoot him in the head and in the heart.

His blood splashes on me.

His heavy body slumps on top of me.

His red head on my head.

Right then, Algerian soldiers storm in.

Kill the two terrorists.

They shove Jim's body aside and put me back in bed.

They left.

I am covered with Jim's blood.

His body is on the floor.

On his stomach.

But his neck is twisted around.

His eyes wide open in his bloodied face stare at me.

—===(0/0/0)===—

The *limpia* session for the third night is coming to an end. Consuelo realizes that Rosa had a difficult time talking about the horrors of the terrorist siege. She decides to stop the session. Rosa seems relieved to swallow a double dose of soporific syrup. Meanwhile Carlos, once more, turns the tape recorder off and organizes his notes. He feels so sad for having heard about his lover's extreme traumas. He never thought that such things could happen.

NIGHT # 4 – Oct 29, 2015 – AT THE US EMBASSY

After a day of total bed rest, Rosa is returned to the makeshift treatment room, for her fourth nightly catharsis. Consuelo and Carlos are anxious. They are concerned that Rosa might describe even worse things than she did on the third night. But they go ahead, hoping for the best.

—⟨ꝯ/ꝯ/ꝯ⟩—

"What is your name, dear. And what do you want to tell us tonight?" said Carlos, according to the prescribed ritual.

"My name is Rosa. Rosa Vasquez."

—⟨ꝯ/ꝯ/ꝯ⟩—

"I do not know what else happened at In Amenas. When I woke up, I was in a different infirmary.

A military female nurse was by my bedside.

She talked to me first in French and then in English. She was nice to me.

"Good afternoon. You are now at the US embassy in Algiers. We are here to take good care of you. We gave you some medicine. You should feel better, pretty soon. First, let's have a snack, shall we?"

Feeling good and refreshed, I ate my pineapple Danish and drank my glass of milk.

—⟨ꝯ/ꝯ/ꝯ⟩—

I stopped counting the days.

I was having a good time. The nurse, a doctor, intelligence officers. Everybody was nice and courteous.

—⌁⌁⌁—

A military psychiatrist came to talk to me many times. He, too was a nice fellow. He asked: "Tell me about your nightmare."

"Jim's head rolls on the floor towards me. The eyes stare at me. The bloodied mouth moans 'Your fault, Rosa. Your fault'," I said

After, he told me : "You have PTSD. We will help you get rid of your nightmares."

—⌁⌁⌁—

The US embassy residence is in a classical Moorish villa. Beautiful gardens. You can see Algiers and its bay.

I was always accompanied and taken care of.

At one time, I was told that I was going to be debriefed by CIA officers.

—⌁⌁⌁—

For the debriefing, a translator was repeating the questions in French. But I understood the English, anyway.

I answered all questions. My name, my profession, my address, my citizenship, people I knew and did not know.

I could not figure why they were not satisfied by my answers.

Sometimes I thought that they were suspecting that I was in cahoots with the terrorists.

They asked me why I was in In Amenas. They wanted to hear all details of what had happened on the road when our party was attacked at the fake checkpoint, by the terrorists, before reaching In Amenas.

I told them that I recollected only what happened on the road. Not the details of what happened at the clinic.

Someone said that they had read the notes taken by the medic. I said: "Yes, Jim!" and I stopped talking.

Then, one day, one of the interrogating officers asked me if I had been known by another name before. "Rose Blanchard," I said. "From my mom Mary Blanchard," I said. They were surprised.

One of them stepped out of the room with a piece of paper.

Another day, they said: "Now, tell us about your dad Paolo Vasquez."

"He was only my step-dad," I said. "Oh yes? and what was the name of your real dad?" "Tarik," I said. "Oh yes? and what was his last name?" "I do not know," I said. "Oh yes? and where was he from?" "He was born in the village of Aït Wufur in Kabylia," I said.

One of the officers stepped out of the room with a piece of paper.

Another day, they asked me if I had ever met my biological dad. I said that he had died before I was born. Killed by the French police in Paris and thrown in a river. "Can you swear that no one from the Algerian secret police ever talked to you or check on you during your twenty years at the University?" "I swear," I said.

For the first time, the intelligence officer seemed to be mad at me. As if I was lying.

"Are you sure? We know of a Tarik from Aït Wufur. Not a bad guy. But we do know of him, in relation to 9/11. This is strange. I accept your word. Sign here. But we might contact you again in the future. Perhaps for a DNA test. Will you accept that?"

"Yes," I said. And I signed a new document.

———✧✧✧———

Another day, three officers kindly took me to a different room. "We have an announcement to make, Professor."

"Yes?" I said.

"We found that your mother Mary Blanchard-Reinhart was an American citizen, married to a Vyktor Reinhart in 1956. Do you know about that?"

"Oh, yes" I said.

"Well, Professor. We are pleased to let you know that you are an American citizen. We are going to issue you a US passport. And then we will accompany you to the US Navy Medical Center in San Diego. For treatment. Even though you are a civilian."

They told me: "We brought you here with the approval of the Algerian authorities. Nobody knew who you were. But the notes taken by the deceased nurse Jim Walker said 'Traumatized. No communication. Unknown origin. Understand English. Likes Hotel California and the name Lovely Face'. So, on a hunch, we decided to bring you here, just to check."

When I heard Jim's name, the nightmare came back. I screamed. I cried.

The nurse took me to my bed. She gave me pills.

That is the way I found myself in San Diego in early February 2013.

Sometime later, I received a letter from the State of California probate. They were telling me that, even though the probate case was closed, according to the will of a deceased Vyktor Reinhart, in favor of a deceased Mary Reinhart-Blanchard or her descendants, I was given access to a two-million-dollar account at Citibank.

Dr. Caldwell treated me for three months, but did not cure my PTSD.

I still had a difficult time with obsessions and nightmares.

I wanted to go to the end of the world. Away from the obsessions.

Dr. Caldwell agreed that it would do me good. "You are an American citizen. You can go wherever you want!"

After seeing a real-estate ad on Facebook, I purchased the La Linda hotel.

And here I am!"

————◎/◎/◎————

The *limpia* session for the fourth night came to a soft end. Consuelo and Carlos feel relieved that nothing worse happened after the terrorist siege. They are happy that Rosa was saved by the Americans. Above all, they now understand why, in November 2013, Rosa arrived in Todos Santos, acting like a zombie. Consuelo comes to realize that poor Rosa was concocting her silly lies to protect herself from those terrible nightmares.

No need for a soporific, tonight.

————◎/◎/◎————

Consuelo gives a motherly kiss on Rosa's forehead.

"Child, the bad spirits have now left your soul, for ever."

Carlos cannot contain his enthusiasm. "Rosa you are cured! Tell me. Some time ago, you told me about Shahrazad. Was she saved the same way?"

"Yes darling. I was saved, like Shahrazad. Over many nights. But in a much better way. You see, after one thousand nights, Shahrazad was indeed saved. But poor gal ended up without a lover. And me, after four nights, I do have a lover. And that lover is you!"

Carlos jumps to kiss his Rosa.

She stands up.

In a strong embrace, they passionately share a burst of tears.

CHAPTER 3

Dia de Muertos and beyond

DIA DE MUERTOS –
Oct 31, Nov 1 and 2, 2015

Rosa's born-again *limpia* four-night therapy was a total success. On top of that, it was perfectly timed, as it smoothly blended with the joyful and mystical Day of the Dead celebrations.

Around the *ofrenda* at home, during the processions; and at the *Panteo Antiguo* [Old Cemetery], prayers to Santa Maria de Guadalupe will give the needed Christian conclusion to Rosa's recovery.

Intuitively Rosa knows that her recovery will become permanent on one condition: that she achieves total one-ness with the Todos Santos locals.

Over the past weeks, preparation for the Dia de Muertos festivities have been going on feverishly. Everybody is involved in Todos Santos, in the whole of Baja, in the whole of Mexico.

From this point on, Rosa will be one of them. One with them.

Gone is the last remnant of 'touristy' pretences.

———✦✦✦———

In private, Carlos had warned her: "This year, we will celebrate at Consuelo's home. There will be a lot of people. Consuelo's family will be there. Carmensita, Juanito and his wife Josefina, and other visiting relatives. People who come and people who go. But the four of us will be the core of the family."

"Four, you say? Consuelo, you, me. That makes three. Who is the fourth?"

"It's Don Pedro I'm talking about. He has no family. All his brothers and sisters are dead. He was the baby of his family...and now he's all alone, at eighty-seven."

———✦✦✦———

As Carlos had explained to Rosa, the Dia de Muertos festivities start at Consuelo's home. Don Pedro's fame in Todos Santos and beyond, create an additional steady stream of visitors who come and go, embrace each other, exchange personal stories about their respective dearly departed. Knowing that these deceased are physically present with them, the celebrants meditate, share tears of joy, sitting around the ofrenda before placing their offerings there.

Next to the photos of the ancestors of the families of Consuelo, Don Pedro and Señor and Señora Gomez, there are three small white cards, delicately put together, on the right. The one from Carlos, declares 'la Guaycura nacion'. The other two, pinned by Rosa, are dedicated to 'Tarik' and 'Mary'.

Carmensita, in front of a modest stove, surrounded by young admirers, is busy around a large pot where dry ground jalapenos, cocoa bean powder and secret spices begin to simmer before turning into 'molle', the ritual dish of the day.

Rosa goes to Consuelo's to whisper a question in her ear. Consuelo's answer is enthusiastic. "Claro que si, hija mia!"

Encouraged by Consuelo's approval, Ourida returns to sit next to Carlos. "Could you run an errand for me?"

"But of course... what do you need?"

"Go to Supermercado Martinez and buy some higo chumbo [prickly pear]. This will be my offering to my dad Tarik. He must certainly have enjoyed eating them in Algeria. They grow wild in Kabylia. And also corn on the cob for my mom Mary. She must have liked eating them at America picnics when she was a kid."

"I'll be going right away. It's a great idea to do this for your parents' souls, honey. I'm going to see if by any chance Carmensita needs anything, for the kitchen."

Carlos is back from the Supermercado Martinez, with the chumbos and corn on the cob.

"Thank you, Carlos. Good thing you found some. Guess what I'm going to tell you."

"You want me to guess what, cariña?"

"For the first time since I arrived here, I know that I am a local. A woman from Magical Todos Santos. I feel deeply peaceful. More than peaceful. Serene ..."

"Wow! Serene? That's a big word! Let me check it in my pocket dictionary," teases Carlos with a big smile. "Whatever it is, here is our decision. We want to see your serenity continue for a long while. We want you to be anchored in our own way of life, its joys and its pains. For a starter, at Don Pedro's suggestion, we are going to immerse you in the Dia de Muertos festivities. The parades, the meetings with the departed around the *ofrendas*, the celebrations around the graves at the *Panteon Antiguo* cemetery. This way, my love, you will be totally bonded in our community. You will not be a foreigner anymore. This will be the natural conclusion to your *limpia*. Be prepared, though! Consuelo herself is in charge of your immersion. You know how she is, right? She will cover absolutely all aspects: cultural, spiritual, emotional."

"You guys are spoiling me!"

"You deserve it, honey."

⸻◦◦◦⸻

After breakfast, Consuelo, Carmensita and Josefina dress the kids in their Dia de Muertos costumes. Carlos, disguised as a highway-robber, paints Rosa's face as a Catrina skeleton.

He gives her a handheld mirror. "See how you look?"

First, Rosa cannot hold a big laugh "Wow! You did a good job on me, sir!" before realizing the incredible change she has gone through. She finally can look at herself in a mirror. The PTSD curse is gone, for sure.

Relieved beyond all hopes, Rosa-Catrina tenderly hugs Carlos-the-highway-robber.

LIFE GOES ON – FROM Nov 3, 2015

It takes a while for the Dia de Muertos excitement to subside. Progressively, life returns to normal at La Nueva Linda, as new batches of giddy newlyweds arrive.

"*Muy bien*, Carlos and Rosa," announces Consuelo for all to hear. "It's time to prepare for the wedding. We have only one month to go. Carmensita, your job is to plan the reception dinner. Rosa, you and I will select your wedding gown. Carlos, you are in charge of the guest list."

"... And the honeymoon ..." giggles Carmensita.

"*Seguro*," dicen Carlos y Rosa simultáneamente.

"*¿Y a donde?*" pregunta Consuelo, con ansiedad.

Carlos concludes "Our honeymoon? Do not worry, Consuelo. In San Diego, that's where we'll go. On top of it all, there will be a big surprise for you all, God willing, isn't that so, Rosa?"

"Yes, Carlos, you are absolutely right!" declares Rosa, before smacking a theatrical kiss on her novio's lips for all to see, applaud and cheer ...

Conclusion

I hope that you enjoyed reading Rosa's story.

She, Carlos, and I tried to share it with you, as vividly as possible.

My personal delight is to have discovered that, thanks to Rosa, Todos Santos is more 'Magical' than it ever was.

Rosa's PTSD story was based on traumatic events that she badly wanted to forget. Most PTSD patients find it impossible to explain their condition to other people. Rosa dared share her struggles and recovery, having found that Life goes beyond the boundaries of rationalism. Trained as a scientist, she discovered that love and communal bonds, combined with age-old mystical beliefs, have curative values that can no longer be ignored. She was lost and now is found.

Coming in the opposite direction, Carlos told us how he sees himself both as the victim and the beneficiary of western rationalism. His personal and uniquely insightful shortcuts across millenaries of human evolution, are stunning. And deserve our thoughtful attention.

Carlos and Rosa's love affair harmoniously blended love and science into a positive experience that could be an eye opener for many of us.

Henry Towers

P.S.: You might be interested to know that our friends got married in December 2015, in Todos Santos. They had planned to enjoy their short honeymoon in San Diego and stay there for a whole year.

Miraculously, their Guaycura twin boys were born in September 2016.

Glossary

You can find a FREE detailed glossary online at
https://www.rosag.bellefontainebooks.com

PTSD - POST-TRAUMATIC STRESS DISORDER

The Post-Traumatic Stress disorder is a psychological disfunction which can develop in persons after being exposed to a traumatizing event, such as:

- Military Combat

- Terrorist attacks

- Sexual aggressions

- Traumatic accidents

PTSD is generally treated with various types of psychotherapy and pharmacotherapy.

PTSD – WHAT IS A FLASHBACK?

A PTSD flashback is the return of a traumatic past experience. It is part of the disorders of the implicit emotional memory.

These involuntary mental images arise suddenly and completely invade the consciousness, without necessarily having any connection with the present situation. They can be triggered by an external stimulus such as a smell, the sight of an object or a sound.

SAN DIEGO: US NAVY HOSPITAL

The Naval Medical Center San Diego (NMCSD), also known as Bob Wilson Naval Hospital, is a highly medicalized facility of the United States Navy. Located on the grounds of Balboa Park in San Diego, the hospital opened its doors over 100 years ago. Its mission has always remained the same: to provide the best medical care to operational forces, their families, and veterans in a family-centered care environment. Organizationally, the hospital operates under military command.

WHERE IS BAJA CALIFORNIA?

Baja California is a Mexican peninsula 775 miles long and 75 miles wide on average. It lies south of the U.S. state of California, of which it is a natural extension.

BAJA CALIFORNIA: HOTEL CALIFORNIA IN TODOS SANTOS

Hotel California was founded in 1948 by a Chinese immigrant named Mr. Wong. An innovator, he turned it into a bar after importing ice from La Paz in the 1950s, along with a bazaar and a gas station, big novelties at the time.

In the 60s and 70s, the hotel became a favorite spot for American hippies and quickly fell into disrepair.

But it had no connection with the rock band Eagles. The Eagles' song "Hotel California" was in no way inspired by Todos Santos' Hotel California.

In 1970, a Canadian couple, John and Debbie Stewart, bought the hotel. They made numerous renovations that won prestigious awards for design and decor that justified its title as a "little gem in the middle of the desert".

BAJA CALIFORNIA: TODOS SANTOS

Located in the foothills of the Sierra de la Laguna Mountains on the Pacific coast of the Baja California peninsula, Todos Santos is close to the Tropic of Cancer.

With a population of 10,000, it has become a very popular tourist destination.

BAJA CALIFORNIA: PREHISTORIC ROCK ART

The Baja California peninsula, in northwestern Mexico has several hundred prehistoric sites, located in the San Francisco Sierra, the San Juan Sierra, the San Borja Sierra and the San Francisco Sierra, including La Trinidad and Pintas Piedras. Some of them are decorated caves or rock shelters, others are deposits of fossil bones from different eras. The region is very rich in cave and rock art.

BAJA CALIFORNIA: LA ZORRA WATERFALL

15 miles from Santiago, the Canyon de la Zorra is a charming place, an oasis that stands out for its beautiful waterfall of sixty feet, plunging into its natural pool.

It is the ideal place to enjoy a moment of relaxation, to refresh yourself after the surrounding climbs.

BAJA CALIFORNIA: THE DAY OF THE DEAD

Dia de Muertos is a Mexican holiday celebrated in Mexico and elsewhere, associated with the Catholic celebrations of All Saints' Day, from October 31 to November 2. During this multi-day holiday, families and friends gather to pray and remember friends and family members who have passed away.

BAJA CALIFORNIA: THE OFRENDA

An ofrenda is a domestic altar with a collection of objects placed on ritual display during the annual and traditionally Mexican celebration of Dia de

Muertos. An ofrenda, which can be quite large and elaborate, is usually created for a deceased person and is intended to be placed on the altar.

BAJA CALIFORNIA: NATIVE AMERICANS

Native to Baja California Sur, the Guaycura are one of the oldest groups in Baja California. The Guaycura were nomadic hunter-gatherers, with a language that cannot be related to any Native American language. For this reason, some researchers believe that the Guaycura have been present in the Baja California Sur region for thousands of years.

NORTH AFRICA: THE BERBERS

The Berbers are the first inhabitants of North Africa. The vast majority of Algerians are of Berber origin. But some tribes have joined the Arab civilization, while others - mainly the Kabyles, the Tuaregs and the Mzabis - have retained their ancestral language and culture, even though they are Muslims.

Today's Berbers are descendants of the prehistoric Saharan civilizations known for their amazing rock paintings discovered especially in the Tassili N'Ajjer National Park in Algeria.

NORTH AFRICA: ROCK ART

Saharan rock art is an important field of archaeological study that focuses on artworks carved or painted on the natural rocks of the central Sahara Desert. Saharan rock art includes many periods beginning around 12,000 years ago.

NORTH AFRICA: THE IN AMENAS TERRORIST ATTACK

The Algerian natural gas extraction facility at In Amenas, located in the southwestern Sahara, is co-owned by an international consortium.

The In Amenas hostage crisis began on January 16, 2013, under the control of a terrorist brigade of Mokhtar Belmokhtar affiliated with al-Qaeda.

The terrorists killed 39 expatriate hostages and one Algerian (for raising the alarm) at the Tiguentourine gas site near In Amenas, Algeria.

One of Belmokhtar's top lieutenants, Abdul al Nigeri, led the attack and was among the terrorists killed.

NORTH AFRICA: MOKHTAR BELMOKHTAR

Mokhtar Belmokhtar is a notorious Algerian thug turned terrorist.

After volunteering in Afghanistan with Bin Ladin against the Russians in 1995, he returned to Algeria and pledged allegiance to Al-Qaeda to carry out terrorist actions in Algeria.

A one-eyed war veteran, he was nicknamed 'Mister Marlboro' for his illicit cigarette trade.

Described as 'untouchable' he made a name for himself by ordering a deadly attack on the internationally run Algerian gas site of In Amenas in January 2013. Four months later, he reportedly masterminded two suicide attacks in Niger, targeting a military base in Agadez and the French-run uranium mine in Arlit, killing at least 25 people.

NORTH AFRICA: THE TIGR

The Tigr (Russian: Тигр) is a Russian all-terrain vehicle used by the Algerian National Army.

NORTH AFRICA: THE PRICKLY PEAR

Imported from Mexico in the 16th century during the colonial era of the Conquistadors, the Opuntia became an invasive plant but also a source of human and animal food all around the Mediterranean basin.

Curiously named 'prickly pear' in French, in reference to the 'Barbary Coast' i.e. present-day Algeria, the fruit is known in Arabic as 'karmous n'sara', in other words 'fig of the Christians'. But on the North African market, it is called 'hindia' (in reference to India, the country that Christopher Columbus thought he had reached in 1492), or 'chumbo', precisely the same term used by the indigenous Amerindians of Mexico! Among the ancestors of the latter, the Aztecs venerated him under the name of Huitzilopochtli.

NORTH AFRICA: THE PIEDS NOIRS PEOPLE

The Pieds-Noirs are people of French and European origin who were born in Algeria during the period of French rule from 1830 to 1962. At the end of the Algerian War of Independence, in a tragic mass exodus of more than one million people, they fled Algeria, mainly to France and Israel.

'HOTEL CALIFORNIA' by the EAGLES rock group

The 1976 Eagles rock band piece 'Hotel California' has been acclaimed worldwide for its brilliant harmonies and innovative instrumental techniques.

But there is no connection with the rock band Eagles and Hotel California of Todos Santos.

Main Characters

Rosa Vasquez

University professor of ethnology in Algeria.

A victim of the In-Amenas terrorist attack in January 2013 in Algeria's Sahara Desert, she suffers from PTSD.

Carlos

Last living member of the Guaycuras, a Native American tribe decimated in Baja California by the Conquistadors, the Jesuits and then the Franciscans missionary orders. Carlos is a self-taught ethnologist.

Carlos and Rosa

After falling in love through their common passion for science, they organize scientific expeditions in pre-historic rock art and get married.

Consuelo

Manager of ' La Linda ', the dilapidated hotel in Todos Santos that Rosa bought in November 2013.

Juanito and Carmensita

Consuelo's son and daughter.

Don Pedro

The shaman Curandero of Todos Santos. At the suggestion of Consuelo and Carlos, Don Pedro treats Rosa for her nervous problems and recommends a special four-night voodoo-like catharsis.

Mary Blanchard

Rosa's American-born mother, a destitute expatriate in Paris.

Tarik

Rosa's Algerian biological father, born in Kabylia's Aït Wufur in Algeria. Presumed dead, it was said he had been killed by the French police during a political demonstration in Paris in January 1961.

Vyctor Rheinhart

First husband of Mary Blanchard. Muscle-man star in Hollywood.

Paolo Vasquez

Adoptive father of Rosa, Pied-Noir of Spanish origin, refugee in Algeria after the defeat in 1939 of the Republican resistance fighters in Spain. In 1962 he became a refugee in France after Algeria's independence. Abusive, alcoholic.

Sebastian

Carlos's childhood friend from the Cochimi Native American tribe of Baja California.

Margarita

Sebastian's wife, she agreed to become the donor for the conception of Rosa's and Carlos' twins.

The Author

Now retired, I like to tell stories that I hope will be pleasant to read while carrying strong messages.

My stories contain some of the lessons I have gleaned over the years.

As a Frenchman born in Algeria, I have lived in a multicultural and multiethnic environment that has seen many socially unstable and destructive periods. Like many others, I have lived through and witnessed the deep traumas caused by international or civil wars as well as by terrorism from all sides.

My goal is to contribute to a greater awareness of PTSD and its impact on hidden human dramas, at the personal as well as the global levels.

The Henry Towers Series

Published in 2008 on Amazon, 'The Torch' is a historical novel in English about the Second World War, covering the period from the American landing in North Africa on November 8, 1942 to the massacres of Setif on May 8, 1945.

The serialized French version of 'The Torch' will be released in January 2023.

Rosa, a Survivor', published by Amazon in December 2020, is the English version of 'Ourida, a Survivor'.

.

www.ingramcontent.com/pod-product-compliance
Lightning Source LLC
Chambersburg PA
CBHW060220180626
46813CB00007B/2897